THE QUARRY

THE
QUARRY

DAMON GALGUT

Atlantic Books
London

First published in 1995 by Penguin Books South Africa (Pty) Ltd.

This revised edition first published in Great Britain in 2004 by Atlantic Books, an imprint of Grove Atlantic Ltd.

1 3 5 7 9 8 6 4 2

A CIP catalogue record for this book is available from the British Library.

ISBN 1 84354 293 5 (Hardback edition)
ISBN 1 84354 294 3 (Trade paperback edition)

Printed in Great Britain by CPD, Ebbw Vale, Wales

Atlantic Books
An imprint of Grove Atlantic Ltd
Ormond House
26–27 Boswell Street
London
WC1N 3JZ

This book was completed
with the financial support of
the Foundation for the Creative Arts.

Thanks also to
Wendy Searle and Robert Hill
for their help.

1

Then he came out of the grass at the side of the road and stood without moving. He rocked very gently on his heels. There were blisters on his feet that had come from walking and blisters in his mouth that had come from nothing, except his silence perhaps, and bristles like glass on his chin.

He crossed to a stone that was next to the road and sat. He was there for a while until, apparently without emotion, he bowed his head and wept into his hands. Then he stopped. He looked around. The road was a curve of dust. On either side of it the grasslands stretched flatly away and there wasn't a solitary tree.

'Jesus H. Christ,' said the man.

He took from his right hip pocket a glass cooldrink bottle which he had filled with brackish water at a stream. He unscrewed the top, spat into the dirt and took a long swallow. He checked the level of the water and screwed the top back on. He put the bottle back into his pocket.

He sat for a while and looked. He stared at the lines on his palm. He started to say something. But it was too hot to speak. He said nothing. He shook his head once briefly, perhaps to shake a fly from his face.

Then he stood and began to move again, tottering down that empty white trail. He looked like a figure fired in a kiln, still smoking slightly and charred. A gull followed him for a while, hovering above his head, white and mewling. He stopped and threw a stone at it and it veered away to one side, tilting on its wings. It vanished over the grass, going towards the sea.

The road curved left. It went up a rise and then he himself could see the water, flat and endless as it moved in on the shore. He wanted to go to it. There was a bed of brittle reeds between the road and the beach and he moved between the dry, crackling stalks. He came to the sand, which was white and fine, marked as though with music by the lines of ancient tides. Shells and weed, skeletons of crabs.

He hung his clothes as he undressed on a piece of salt-whitened driftwood that stuck up out of the sand. His clothing was a peculiar mixture of articles. The boots looked military and so did the socks. His shirt was red cotton with irregular white buttons and had been pilfered in passing from some nameless settlement somewhere. The blue pants were likewise stolen from a washing-line near the city. He took them off and then he was naked in the cold wash of sun. His body was bizarrely quilted in areas of sunburn and whiteness, cleanness and dirt. He was a harlequin.

He went down to the water. There were gulls eddying above him again. He ignored them. He waded out a little way till the water reached his knees. It was cold.

He washed himself. There was a quality to his movements that was perfunctory and detached so that all activity was one. Crying or washing, it was the same to him. He scooped hand-fuls of the freezing water over his back, his face. He scoured his skin with sand. Then he waited for a time with his hands at his sides and gazed at the thin shell of the horizon which seemed inscribed in ink and which curved across all he could see of the world.

He went back to the beach. His clothes were where he'd left them, hanging on the piece of driftwood, and for a few moments he looked at these pieces of cloth with surprise. He had no memory of leaving them there and it seemed to him for a moment that they belonged to someone else. Then he remembered. He dressed again slowly, the material sticking to the damp places on his skin. The clothes smelled of something or someone or maybe of nothing.

He walked back through the reeds to the road. He went on walking north towards what he didn't know.

In the late afternoon he came on another figure like him that was moving in the other direction, south. As they drew opposite each other on that empty road they stopped. Now that he stood near another human form it could be seen that he was a big man, very tall. The other man was black, wearing a dark blue suit. They looked at each other warily.

He decided to speak.

'Hello,' he said.

The other man nodded, carefully.

'Where does this road go?' he said.

The other man smiled, inscrutably.

'Do you know where I can find water?'

He took the bottle from his pocket to show him.

At this the other became voluble. He was pointing back the way he'd come. He spoke while he did, but in a language the first man didn't understand. It was high-pitched and rapid. Then he fell silent again and stood still. They looked at each other.

'Goodbye,' he said.

The other man nodded and smiled. 'Goodbye,' he said, pronouncing the word laboriously.

They went on their way. They drew slowly away from each other on the pale white road, casting backward glances at each other, like two tiny weights on a surface connected to each other by intricate pulleys and dependent on one another for their continuing motion. Then the black man disappeared around a bend. The road went on, unwinding.

Towards evening he saw a tiny settlement of huts in the distance. Perhaps the other man had come from here. They were a way off to the left, at the sea, and he went down from the road and walked towards them. They were fisherman's cottages with walls painted white and he could see boats pulled up on the sand. There were children playing in the gravel outside the houses and they stopped and looked at him with dull amazement as he advanced on them out of nowhere. A yellow dog barked at him and another took up the sound and it was in a cacophony of barks and howls that he came into that place and stood at the edge of it, swaying slightly.

Later some men offered him food and for a short while he parleyed with them, crouched on his heels next to a fire, his shadow cast behind him in stuttering, pantomimic elongation along the ground. A wind was coming up and the clouds that were rising earlier were heavy now and lit from within by jarring concussions of light. They shared their fish with him and he ate with his fingers. They offered him beer but he drank water instead from an oily creek at the edge of the cluster of houses. They didn't ask him his business, where he came from or to where he was going. He spoke little to them. They were curious people, roughened by sun and wind, and their faces were seamed and unknowable under their tight woollen caps. They offered him a bed for the night but he declined politely and set off again into the dark, leaning now into the wind with a tall and plum-coloured sky revealed in explosions of light.

It started to rain soon after. He walked for a while in the silver sheets of water with wind punching him like a fist, but soon came to a culvert under the road. There was water running through it but he found a dry place inside and curled up with a gratitude that he had never felt for any other bed. He slept with a tiredness that was close to death. The storm passed and the clouds went on, passing over the sea. Some night animal invisible except for the scarlet fissures of its eyes came to the mouth of the culvert and stared at him and went on. He slept on, beyond the memory of dreams, and didn't even twitch in his sleep.

When he woke it was still dark and he came crawling out of the culvert and stretched at the side of the road. The sky was vast and dark and taut and carried in it the myriad points and tracks of stars. He drank water again from a pool at the mouth of the culvert and then set off at that same relentless pace with the sky beginning to whiten on his right. He passed what might have been a farmhouse in the distance with a single light, itself a star, burning in one window and the slow and torpid shapes of labourers bestirring themselves outside. Then the sun, which is also a star, came up as it perhaps always will and the light and heat of it grew across the earth tremendously.

It was good, then, to be walking amid grass that was coloured like roses and air that was soft on the skin. The ground was no longer entirely flat and hillocks rose subtly around him. He passed a tree but it disappeared behind him and no other took its place.

Then the sun was climbing and the air lost its softness and there was no shade. He was going more slowly now than yesterday and there was a roughness to his joints that made it difficult to move. He tried to whistle but no tune came to him and his mouth was too dry, so he stopped. His thoughts were weightless now, unfettered to his life. A small animal of some kind, a mongoose perhaps, squirted softly across the road ahead of him and disappeared into the grass and he didn't stop. There were distant high calls from birds and termite hills rose here and there like citadels that might once have ruled the world and he went on as though to stop would be to cease altogether.

When he heard the sound ahead, he did not hesitate but went into the grass on the right and closed the yellow sheaves behind him like a curtain. He crouched there on the earth that was hard but warm like the living flesh of some basking reptile and looked out through a gap in the stalks at a small patch of road perhaps ten metres wide and listened to the noise of the engine get closer and louder till it filled and passed through that empty space before him that arena as small and charged as the stage of a theatre and had a vision brief but potent of a blue *bakkie* in the front of which sat a florid farmer in short sleeves and hat and next to him his fat dour-faced wife and in the back on two metal drums a labourer lying in bone-breaking repose all three of them rendered in perfect profile as though by the brush of a manic painter who was visionary and occasionally brilliant but almost certainly mad. Then the car was gone and there was dust and the grass was shaking. He saw no reason to proceed but slid sideways to the ground and made himself comfortable and was almost instantly asleep as though expunged by some external dispassionate force that erased his mind like a chalk sketch on a blackboard. He dreamed this time but of things long ago that he didn't know he remembered.

When he awoke this time night was falling and it was under that same but imperceptibly shifted pattern of stars that might mean everything and perhaps nothing at all that he continued on his way, walking now with a motion stiff-legged and strange as though he were partly constructed from straw. Tiny flashes of fire of alien bodies burning as they fell occasionally passed by overhead. He remembered that he was supposed to make a wish but no wish came to him. He walked. Night passed above and he continued to go north at his pace that grew slower and slower. The moon rose at some time before dawn and hung lopsidedly ahead of him like something to which he aspired but then the sun came up and the moon faded till it was merely an outline. He walked as yesterday in the gathering light and heat but felt nothing today of the grace that had infused him. There was a sense inside him of events winding down of springs uncoiled and of wheels slowing and he knew that in his blue and spectral fugue of movement and sleep he was quickly drawing near to the uttermost edge of things.

Then once again he heard the sound of a car behind him. He went as yesterday into the grass at the side of the road but there was a fence here marking the edge of someone's property. He tangled himself on a piece of barbed wire and by the time he got free there was a cut on one finger that made blood run brightly into his palm. Shit, he said. Shit. He crouched on the ground and stared down at his hand that was marked in this way. By now the car was almost on him and he listened to the noise of the engine and waited for it to pass. But it did not pass. It swelled and drew opposite the place where he lay concealed and then stopped. He lay in silence, listening. He heard a car door open and feet crunching in the road. There was a pause and then a man's voice uttered some word and he heard the door being opened. Something metal was lifted out and there were other sounds then.

He couldn't see the road today and he didn't know who might be there or how many of them there were. But he also knew that the next time he lay down would be the last. There was no reason to hide any more. He stood up slowly and emerged from the grass into the road. He stood there, looking down.

The car was a white Toyota. A thick-set man with a balding skull was crouched down at the rear wheel, which was flat. He wore circular golden spectacles that enlarged his eyes. He was perhaps forty years old.

He stood up, this man, on bowed legs. He seemed about to run. But the moment passed and neither of them moved.

Then the driver spoke.

'What do you want?' he said.

The traveller tried to reply but his tongue felt limp and charred and he couldn't make it work. He wanted to eat and drink and he enacted an expressive mime.

The driver shook his head. Then he looked around and back at the man and sighed.

'Just wait,' he said. 'All right?'

The traveller stood in that same place and waited while the driver got down wheezing again into the road and went about changing the tyre. He waited while the other loaded the flat tyre into the boot. Then the side door was opened for him. On the way around the car to the passenger seat the traveller looked into the back and saw boxes and packages piled up and, draped carefully over them, a garment of distinctive colour and cut from which he inferred that the second man was a minister. He got in and the minister shut the door and went back around to his side. He got in too and shut his door. He started the engine.

Now they drove on at speed with the road unspooling through that landscape of grass in which nothing moves except what you dream up in it.

2

A short distance afterwards they came to a garage and tea-room that were near a cluster of houses. They parked the car at the edge of the concrete and got out.

As they walked over the minister tried to support the man's arm but he shook him off.

'Leave me,' he said. 'I can do it.'

'All right,' said the minister. 'All right.'

They went into the tea-room. There was nobody in it except an elderly woman sitting behind the counter. She had blue veins like cryptic runes in her arms and under her stare that was filled with a nameless rage they crossed to a plastic table at the window. There was a lot of plastic in the room.

A black woman in a stained yellow dress came out from the kitchen. She carried a notebook and pen. She was ponderous. The man knew what he wanted but he couldn't speak. He pointed to something on the menu and she wrote in her notebook. She took the minister's order too. Then she went back into the kitchen.

They sat in silence, waiting for their food. The man was looking down at the table. The minister sat back and his eyes, which were molten and dark, flickered all the time on the face of the man. What he thought was never spoken.

'Here's the food,' he said at last.

The same ponderous woman brought it in. She carried it on a tray and put their plates down in front of them and went out. The minister had ordered a cup of coffee. The man was having a full breakfast.

He ate with a voraciousness and speed that were frightening. Still nothing was said. There was the clash of the knife and fork and the sound of his chewing and the old woman behind the counter sat glaring, venting on their strangeness all the insidious fury that she'd gathered up to herself in her life.

When he had finished he pushed back from the table.

'Can I have some more?'

The minister half smiled. 'Go ahead,' he said, waving one hand listlessly.

The man signalled to the old woman, who spoke peremptorily sideways into the kitchen. In due course the other woman came out, carrying on a plate the same breakfast, identically arranged. She put it down in front of him and went out.

This time when he'd finished he again sat back and watched the minister sipping at his coffee. The light that came in through the window had moved on a little and dust motes were visible around them.

'Are you feeling better?'

'Yes,' he said. 'Much better.'

'Do you want to…?'

'I don't want anything,' he said.

They sat there for a bit.

'You wouldn't have a razor and some soap I could borrow?'

The minister took the car key from his pocket. He gave it to the man. 'In the cubby-hole,' he said.

He got up and went out. The garage was deserted except for the pump attendant who was reclining on a cement island with the blue cap of his uniform pulled down over his eyes. The man opened the car and took a small black toiletries bag out of the cubby-hole. He looked again at the minister's frock that was so carefully draped across the back. He shut the door and on his way around the car surreptitiously looked down at the registration. It was a number from a town the man didn't know.

The toilets were behind the tea-room. On his way past the window he glanced in at the minister, who was still sitting at the table. They looked at each other through the glass as though they'd never seen each other before.

In the little alley-way next to the tea-room there was a large red motorbike parked. There wasn't any sign of the rider, but when he got into the bathroom he saw that one of the cubicles was occupied. He filled a basin with water and removed from the black bag the intimate tools required for shaving. He felt weak and as he looked at himself in the foggy mirror it struck him that this activity was ludicrous. He laughed shortly, then stopped.

While he shaved and looked at himself in the glass he thought about everything that had happened. He dried his face and was about to brush his teeth with his finger when he thought what the hell and used the minister's toothbrush instead. He combed his hair with the minister's comb, which had strands of the other man's hair woven into the teeth. He took off his shirt and washed himself and used some deodorant that made him smell like the other man. Then he put all the things he had used back into the bag.

He was about to go out when he caught sight of his hand and saw traces of blood on it. He didn't know where the blood had come from. Then he remembered the barbed wire and turned the tap on and washed off the blood.

The toilet in the cubicle behind him flushed and a man came out. He was about thirty-five years old with black hair cut very short and a manicured moustache. A plump mouth with pink lips, prominent front teeth. In the centre of his forehead there was a round perfect mole. He carried a motorbike helmet. They nodded at each other in the mirror.

'*Warm*,' the newcomer said. He had a high, thin voice.

The man grunted. It was only now that his mind went back to the tea-room and he remembered a pay-phone hanging on the wall. It occurred to him that the minister might be using this phone at the present moment. But when he was back in the car-park he could tell at a glance that the minister hadn't moved from his place at the table.

He put the bag away and looked again at that frock, that garment, on the seat. He touched it with one finger, then shut the door and walked back into the tea-room.

3

The minister's name was Frans Niemand. He was forty-three. He'd come to the church only later in his life, seven and a half years before. Prior to that he'd worked as a clerk in government offices in Paarl. It wasn't, he said, 'the sort of work to make you happy'.

The man watched him. 'Being in the church makes you happy?'

'Do you find that hard to believe?'

'I'm not very… religious.'

They were sitting in their places as they had been before, opposite each other at the low plastic table. Against the glass beside them fat black flies were bashing at the pane. The minister was smoking a cigarette.

The man was thin but not slight. He did not make unnecessary movements though he was clearly capable of speed.

The minister offered him a cigarette. He shook his head.

'So where are you going to now?'

The minister said the name of a town.

'Where's that?'

'Further up the coast. The middle of nowhere. I'm replacing the minister at the mission station there.'

'I didn't know they still had mission stations.'

'Oh, *ja*. Everywhere.'

The woman in the stained yellow dress was back now, standing over them and breathing audibly. A name tag pinned skewly across her bosom said that her name was Beauty. Beauty put down their bill on the table-top and spoke the amount out loud. The minister took the money from his pocket and gave it to her and she counted it and went back into the kitchen.

'Thanks.'

'That's okay.' The minister looked around. 'Shall we go?'

The man nodded but for some reason neither of them moved. The only sound in the room came from a television in the corner. He glanced around and at one of the other tables he saw the man who had come out of the cubicle in the toilets. The motorbike helmet was on top of the table next to him. He was staring intently into space.

He became aware that the man was looking at him and he turned his eyes.

The man looked at the minister. He watched him. He felt the minister wanted something from him.

'Where are *you* going to?'

He thought for a second. He said, 'north,' and started playing with a plastic spoon on the table.

'On foot?'

'Yes, on foot.'

'Where did you start from?'

'You want to know a lot.'

'I answered *your* questions.'

'Shall we go?'

The minister gave a high, girlish laugh. He dabbed at his mouth with a napkin.

'Yes,' he said. 'Let's go.'

They got up from the table and walked across the room while the old woman at the counter who had yet to do anything to justify her presence glared at them with that viciousness that bordered on ebullition. They went out. The petrol attendant was still sleeping outside and a dog was nosing at a bin and they went back to the car and got in. They drove out and back on to the dust road and carried on driving north.

They came to a town half an hour later. They drove down the main street with its leaning lamp-posts and newspapers blowing and its quality of granular light. At a traffic light they stopped and both looked to the right and there was a policeman on the corner. His uniform was blue with noticeable buttons and his face made from some clotted clay. He looked at them and they at him and then both of them looked at each other. The light changed and they drove on and presently left the town behind. The road was close to the sea still and the water stretched immensely away. There was *fynbos* on either side of the car and a light, sour breeze made the branches tremble.

4

Later they came to a fork in the road. The right fork went inland and up to the border. The left went to the minister's destination. They went left. Now the road was colourless and thin as it had been when the man was walking on it. It travelled on within sight of the sea on the left. There were no more houses now and no more people and the sky pressed vacantly down.

It was early afternoon and the sun was hot as they drove. They passed the carcass of an animal next to the road on which three black crows were feeding and one of them flapped up ahead of the car and lumbered off over the veld. The road went through a salt pan that was cracked like a mirror and in which there was nothing alive. There were river beds that were dry. Boulders glistened occasionally from side to side with that fulsome pinkness of flesh.

They came to a quarry on the right that had been mined for chalk but was now abandoned and disused. Ahead of them the road mounted a rise. The minister pulled over. There was an acre of gravel at the edge of the quarry with bunches of scrub growing nearby. The minister parked here, facing away from the road, and switched off the engine. There was silence again, broken only by the faint buzzing of some insect. Then even that fell silent.

The minister took a map out of the cubby-hole. He spread it out across his lap. 'I think we're almost there,' he said. He rolled the map up again and put it away.

They didn't talk for a while. The sun was just past the vertical and it cut hotly into the car. Dust swirled in a sudden complex eddy and faded softly again. The road behind them was deserted and silent. The man could not imagine he had ever walked on it.

'I thought we might have a little drink,' the minister said.

'A little drink of what?'

The minister gave again that leering smile and reached into the back and took out a bottle of wine that was supposed to be used for communion. He opened it with a corkscrew and took a long swallow and handed it to the man. The man sipped too.

'I saw a helicopter this morning,' said the minister.

'Oh, yes,' the man said. He didn't look interested.

'A police helicopter.'

'Yes?'

There was a pause.

'I saw some police cars on the road too. Maybe they were looking for somebody.'

'Maybe,' said the man. He drank from the bottle.

'Who knows?'

'Who knows?' the man said. He gave the bottle back to the minister. He was looking outside the car.

'But that was a long way back,' the minister said.

'Yes.'

A silence fell. The minister leaned towards him and put a hand on his arm.

'You can talk to me. You can tell me everything.'

'You do a lot of that, minister? Listening to people confess?'

'People tell me a lot, yes. It's part of the job.'

Without looking down, the man took the moist hand from his arm.

The minister was sweating. He emitted again that high, awful laugh and he took the bottle and drank. The hole in front of them went down into the earth and there were striations in the rock that had been made visible and the two men who were bound together by some intimate and private communion of their own that neither understood although each believed he did and that would kill both of them in time passed the bottle between them and took sips from it and became gradually drunker as the afternoon went by. They sat with their feet up on the dashboard. Several hours passed in this way. Then the sun had moved on and the shadows of things were stretching along the ground. In the little white car at the edge of the vast hole the two men had finished the first bottle of wine and had opened a second one and the minister was smoking a cigarette that sent lines of smoke across his face. A bird flew over the quarry and for an instant its shadow was cast in bizarre configuration across the scarified ridges of rock, monstrous and segmented and flawed.

The minister put out his cigarette. His eyes were bloodshot. In a hoarse voice, whispering, he said:

'Why don't you give up?'

The man looked at him. The minister's hand was back on his arm now and he could feel its heat.

'Give yourself up. Whatever you've done. They'll find you. In the end.'

Now the minister's hand was fumbling across his chest and was plucking at buttons and breath was roaring in his ear. The minister smelled like milk slightly off and his face was distended on some inner hunger. The man opened his door and got out. He walked to the edge of the quarry. He stood there, looking down. In his arms he carried the second bottle of wine, nearly empty. His shoulders were shaking badly. His face was bloodless and haggard. He said something inaudible. Then he raised his head and spoke aloud:

'They'll get me,' he said.

Just that. The words were simple and heavy. He looked down again. There were boulders at the bottom of the quarry and trees warped into crazed curious shapes and what appeared to be holes in the earth. He could see no clear path down and it was a wonder to him how men had ever mined this hole.

The minister got out of the car too. On bowed unsteady legs he came lurching over to where the man was standing. He enfolded him from behind in a slovenly embrace and started tugging at his buttons again.

The man pulled the fingers from his chest and prised open the arms. He turned.

'You owe me,' the minister said.

'I don't owe you.'

'I bought you food. I gave you a lift.'

'And so?'

The minister looked wildly at him, his face blurred with misery and liquor. 'All I want,' he said, 'all I want… is a little… '

He didn't finish.

'I can't help you,' the man said.

The minister's face sealed whitely like a clam. 'I could tell them,' he said. 'When I get there.'

The man was looking down, into the bottom of the hole. Very flatly, he said: 'Will you?'

The minister swallowed. He wet his lips with his tongue. 'No,' he said.

'No?'

'No. I know what it feels like. To be desperate.'

The man smiled, bitterly and privately. He was still looking down.

'Come on,' the minister said.

'All right,' the man said. He said it softly and was talking to himself but the minister understood him wrongly. He looked at the man and with his hands stretched out stepped forward to touch him again.

The man was holding the bottle by the neck and he raised it

to one side and brought it down with force on the side of the minister's head. He fell sideways, twitching. The bottle broke in mid-air where the minister's head had been and the wine exploded redly, like blood. Or perhaps it was blood. Then the man bent and picked up a rock that had lain untouched here till now and brought it down on the skull of the man below him and stove it in.

The minister was quite dead then. He lay transfixed by an extremity of stillness and only the dust bore witness to his final convulsion in an etching of scuff-marks and lines. The man straightened up as if after long labour and put one hand on his back. He looked around. The sun was almost on the horizon and it had cooled into a red coin but of what currency or what value the man didn't know and he walked to a log nearby and sat. He bowed his head into his hands again and hunched forward and seemed about to cry. But he didn't cry.

5

The landscape around him was lit in a strange unearthly glow and the sky had the quality of metal cooling.

From far back on the dust road there came the sound of an engine. It drew gradually closer. He took the minister under the arms and started to drag him backwards on the ground. He was heavy. His heels bounced. He pulled him behind a termite hill that rose with stalagmitic elegance towards nothing and propped him up like a doll.

The motorbike went past without slowing. The man was also crouched down behind the termite hill, but he could see a flash of red in passing and a leaning figure poised above it. He straightened up. The motorbike went over the rise ahead and the noise of the engine faded. Its dust hung thickly over the road, drifting. He bent down and took the minister under the arms again and dragged him.

He went to the edge of the quarry. A rock slide had made a treacherous slope here and he began to go down. It wasn't possible any more to drag the minister behind him and he gathered him up to his chest and tried to walk sideways, stepping from stone to stone. A rock turned underfoot and he collapsed backwards suddenly, grazing his shoulder. He cursed and struggled upright again, wrestling with the minister. He was staggering downward, downward.

He came to the bottom of the slope. He was covered with sweat by now, and shivering, and weeping a little. He laid the minister down gently across a stone and ran a little way to one side to see how to go on. He made out a vague track that ran like a weal down this side of the quarry and like a man possessed ran back to his charge and dragged him again.

His arms hurt. He followed the track but after a while he couldn't go on. The track disappeared down a vertical face and he stood at the top of this drop and looked out. There was no way to do it except by jumping from one boulder to another but he couldn't jump with the minister on his back. He sat down to think about this. Then there didn't seem another way and with a sort of appalled despair he hauled the body to the edge and dropped it.

It plunged in a white rush and vanished. He heard the sound as it landed. He followed by jumping from one rock to another. He came to the last rock and slid down on his back. He walked down a bank overgrown with weeds. He went through a narrow defile and emerged into a subterranean garden. It was dank and cool here, profuse with random growth. He stood for a while, just breathing.

He was at the bottom of the quarry. He looked up at the brink on which he had been standing half an hour before. Now he was here. The body of the minister lay nearby. He went to it. It had marks and contusions from its fall. He rolled it over and began to undress it. It was a curious task. Shoes socks pants shirt underpants vest: he took them off and folded them into a pile and stacked them neatly close by. The minister was gross in his nudity and lay bared there like some vast, fantastic slug.

The man went away from him and started to look for a place to put him. There were shallow depressions and holes but nothing that resembled a grave. Then he found a deep hole. It went down into the ground and there were stones lying scattered at the bottom.

He went back to the minister. For the last time he dragged him by the arms. He took him to the edge of the hole and tipped him. He fell and lay there, stiffening. The man jumped down next to him. He covered the body with rocks. It took a long time and his arms were weak and it was getting dark by the time he was finished. The first stars were showing overhead.

He climbed out of the hole again and stood there, looking down. He was breathing heavily and sweating. The rocks were piled in a pyramidal shape as if they were paying homage to something. He walked twice around the hole, but it was too dark to see properly.

Less than an hour had passed since he had swung the bottle. Now as he stood here he experienced time flowing backwards from this moment to that as an attenuated continuum that couldn't be measured and it seemed absolutely possible that a day or a year or years had gone by. His hands were shaking again. He turned and walked back through the underground garden. Across the cliff-face at the western side of the quarry there was a vine growing. It had dark-green prolific leaves and there were blue flowers on it that gave off a scent. He picked one.

He started to climb back out of the quarry. He couldn't remember any more how he'd come down and it was too dark now to see properly. When he'd gone a little way he remembered the minister's clothes. He swore. He went back down and got them and began climbing again.

It was full night now. A cold wind was blowing in from the sea and he could smell salt on the air. He emerged from the quarry at a point almost opposite where he'd started and he had to walk back along the edge, stumbling and lurching in hollows. The sound of frogs came up out of the hole, magnified and quavering on stone. He couldn't balance himself. His head was hurting and the muscles in his legs and arms felt powerless and lame. He got to the car. It stood there, glimmering whitely in the dark, both the front doors open.

He went to the car. He took out the black robe. He put it on over his clothes. It was meant for somebody much shorter but fatter than him, so that the length was approximately correct. He unpicked the hems and in a scattering of fine thread added several millimetres to it. He walked in it, looking down at himself in the weak glow of the headlamps. He wasn't laughable. He was haggard and mad and remarkable. He spoke the name of the minister aloud. He paced around, wearing the blue flower in his hair, the wind coming up and the grass hissing.

He took the cassock off again and threw it into the back and got into the car. The seat had been moulded to the contours of a different body and it felt strange underneath him. The key was in the ignition with a metal loop hanging from it from which depended in turn three other keys to doors he would never go through.

He sat for a while behind the wheel, breathing fast. The first bottle emptied of its contents lay spent and transparent at his feet. There was a film of dust on everything in the car as though it had been standing there for years. He stared ahead through the windscreen. There were the corpses of beetles shattered on the glass and their legs and feelers were composed in attitudes of violent expiry.

6

It didn't take long to reach the town. On the far side of the rise beyond the quarry the road flattened out again and then swung inland and bent sharply left towards the sea. A railway track appeared next to the road. At first he couldn't see anything. Then a dim scattering of lights appeared in front of him and there were buildings against the sky.

He pulled over at the edge of the road and again got out of the car. He stood there, looking. There was a road sign leaning nearby with three neat bullet holes punched through it. A piece of newspaper tumbled past in the wind. The town was like a ghostly carnival in the distance and he stared at it for a while. Then he got back into the car and put it in gear and drove on.

The town was small and dispersed and ugly. A barrenness of concrete prevailed. The main streets had been tarred long ago but the side-streets were made from gravel. Nothing was taller than one storey. He passed a café, a butchery, a hair salon. Then he was up against the sea. A metal boom stopped him from driving any further and down the length of a rotting wooden quay he saw the massive shifting outlines of fishing boats at berth. He turned around. He had driven the length of the town and he hadn't seen a single other person.

He parked outside the café. At the till inside there was an overweight man, chewing gum, leaning with one elbow on a dirty fridge. The man nodded to him. There was no response.

'I was looking for the church,' he said.

The man behind the till pointed. He went out. He drove again through the deserted streets with their intermittent spectral lamps burning. It was nine o'clock in the evening.

At a cross-roads he came to the church. It was made of wood and brick and had been newly painted white and its steeple rose tapering on the sky. He parked outside and got out. The doors were closed and there was no light inside. He walked behind the building and there was a large house there and voices came from inside. The door was stencilled out in light.

He went to the door and knocked. While he waited he thought that he was about to fall over and he steadied himself on the wall. There were tiny motes moving in front of his eyes and his mouth felt papery and dry.

The door was opened by a woman. She had a blonde beehive of hair. She had no eyebrows but she had drawn a horizontal stroke with a pencil above each eye. In the centre of her forehead there was a round perfect mole.

He said to her: 'I want the minister's house.'

'My husband is the minister.'

He looked at her. Something in his appearance had frightened her. She had taken several steps back.

'I'm the new minister,' he said.

She stared at him.

'Oh,' she said. 'Oh.' She smiled. It was clear that she was relieved. 'You want the *other* church.'

'The other church?'

'The mission church. The one in the township.' She came out to the car with him to show him. 'Keep going,' she told him. 'Keep on.'

'Thank you.'

There was a white dog barking shrilly at her feet. She picked it up and held it and stroked it. It had a small bow on its head. '*Bly stil, liefie,*' she said.

He drove on. She receded into the gloom behind, holding her struggling white dog.

The road that she had pointed out to him ran to the northern end of the town and then went on. The houses with their grey rectangles of lawn disappeared behind. The road was untarred. The car was jolting on ruts and he couldn't see anything in the headlights except grass leaning and flowing in the wind. He was looking for a place in which to turn around when a figure took shape ahead. He stopped and hooted. The figure turned. It was a man.

'Is this the road to the township?'

'Ja. Ja. Ja.'

'Can you tell me how to get to the church?'

'I can show you the church.'

'Get in.'

He did. There was a strong smell of drink in the car. They drove on. A little way ahead the road came to the township. There was debris. He saw people sitting here and there in doorways or standing in groups on corners. They turned their heads to look at him.

He felt a strange uneasiness. 'Why are they staring?'

The other man laughed. 'They're looking at the car,' he said.

'There aren't a lot of cars?'

'No, my *broer*,' he said. 'Turn here.'

In the centre of the township there was a huge cement plaza with cracks and flaws running through it and at one end of it there was a prefabricated building with sandbags piled up in front. On the other side, facing it, the church. It was squat and low with holes gaping in the brickwork and only by a dislodged cross canted skewly on its summit did he know it for what it was. He parked.

'Thanks,' he said. 'What's your name?'

'Valentine.' He was looking at the cassock. 'Are you a minister?'

The man shifted. 'No,' he said. He didn't know why he'd said it. They got out.

'What about my luck?'

Holding out his hand.

The man shook his head. 'I've got nothing,' he said.

'*Ag*, brother. I showed you the church, my brother.'

'I've got nothing,' he said. It was true.

'Goodnight, my *broertjie*.'

He said nothing. He stood next to his car and watched Valentine go diagonally across the plaza. When he reached the far side he disappeared between a café and an empty lot.

The man turned. There were no lights in this church either, no sign of anyone nearby. He went to the wooden door and pushed, but it was locked. He went to the side of the church. There was a house here and he went to the door and knocked. It was opened in a moment by a woman. They looked at each other.

'I'm Reverend Niemand,' he said.

7

She was wearing a long flannel bathrobe with tiny faded flowers on it. It was tied at the waist but it looked to him as if there was nothing underneath it. Fine bones and shadows and skin.

She stood aside for him to enter and he came in and she closed the door. He was at the head of a passage that went off towards an open door at the end. There was another door, closed, halfway down. To his right he could see a room that seemed to be a kitchen. There was a table with a plate of half-eaten food on it and a glint of knives and forks lying around.

'We've been waiting for you,' she said.

'Yes. I was… delayed. On the way.'

He followed her down the passage. There was linoleum on the floor and there was wallpaper on the walls that had faded till it was almost invisible. His room was the one at the end of the passage, so small that if he had fallen in it his head would have struck the far wall. There was a window that looked out on the plaza. There was a bed, a small desk, a chair. There was a wooden crucifix on the wall.

'I hope it'll be all right here,' she said.

Her voice was cool and polite but felt empty to him as if it were nothing but words. He sat down on the bed. He hadn't seen or touched a bed or a blanket for three and a half weeks now and he ran a hand slowly over the fibres, feeling them. He heard her voice speaking again and it said you have blood on your clothes.

He looked down. He saw that there were vivid red stains on the front of his shirt and a smear on the leg of his pants. He stared at these marks for a moment with surprise. Then he looked up at her.

'It's because of... because of this.'

He showed her the cut on his finger.

'But you must clean that.'

She took his hand in hers. He became aware that it was trembling violently and pulled it away.

'I cut it on a piece of wire. Next to the road. When I stopped.'

'It's a deep cut.'

'I know,' he said. 'I know. Yes, you're right. I must clean it. I'll do it now.'

Still she would not leave the room.

'I'm very tired,' he said.

'Don't you have a bag? A suitcase or something?'

'In the car.'

'You must get it,' she said. 'It's not safe there.'

'I'll get it,' he said. He didn't move.

Eventually she went out, but she came back in again almost immediately with a bowl of water and a cloth and some Dettol. She set them down next to the bed.

'For the cut.'

'I'll do it now,' he said.

A glance passed between them. She was a middle-aged woman, slightly underweight, with veins showing in her forehead. Her eyes were a crystalline blue. There was something in her movements that was wary and watchful and he felt remotely afraid.

'I've already eaten,' she said. 'But I can get something for you.'

'I just want to sleep,' he said. 'It's the journey.'

'Yes,' she said.

She went out, closing the door. He sat for a long time on the bed. He remembered that she had told him to unpack the car and he knew he had to get up and do it. But from somewhere inside him a lassitude was rising and threatening to envelop his brain. He lay down sideways across the bed with his feet still resting on the floor and his hands pillowed under his head. Just for a minute, he thought. Just for one minute. He heard voices speaking elsewhere in the house or maybe they were speaking in him. He closed his eyes and began to breathe deeply and when he woke again it was morning. The car had been burgled in the night.

8

They had broken one of the side windows at the back. There was a half-brick lying on the seat and a fine dusting of glass. Except for a single sock that lay curled on the floor there was nothing left in the car. All the boxes with the minister's possessions in them, the clothes, the papers, the books, all gone. The seat looked naked. He stood there, looking at it. He felt that he should do something, that some action was required of him, but he didn't know what he should do.

It was early in the day and a thin wash of sunlight came down. There were people crossing the plaza, going about their business, and one or two of them had stopped to watch him. A stranger unexpectedly among them. He turned his back and leaned on the car. Thinking what must I do. He bowed his head and suddenly he smelled himself, sweat dirt smoke intermingled, all the complex odours of flight. On the front of his shirt and the leg of his pants the bloodstains. He raised his head and looked up.

She was there. She had come out of the house while he stood there. She was wearing the flannel robe still with its faded impress of flowers and she came walking across the concrete towards him without any shoes on. His feet were also bare. She stopped next to him and both of them stood looking at the car.

'I told you...' she said.

He said nothing. He bent down and picked up that single useless sock from the floor and twisted it round in his hand.

'I'll get Captain Mong,' she said.

'Captain Mong?'

'He's the one in charge.'

She gestured across the plaza at the prefabricated building he had seen last night with the sandbags piled up in front of it and a flag hanging limply from a pole. He looked back at her but she wasn't going across the plaza. She was going back to the house.

In a moment he followed. The door to her room was closed. He went down the passage to his room and stood there, looking around him. There was the desk and the chair and the bed on which he had slept. They didn't seem familiar to him. He stood there, rubbing his arms. He heard voices behind him in the house and he closed the door of the room and pressed his ear to the wood. Listened. A door, her door, opened. Feet went quickly down the passage. He went to the window and saw the woman emerging from the house. A policeman in uniform was behind her and they walked together to the car.

He moved back behind the curtain and again stood rigid and immobile. His hands trembling. He felt events and objects thickening in collusion against him and began to tear at his clothes. Then the action took on meaning and he got undressed very quickly and threw the clothes down on the bed. His body was long and pale, like a blade. Naked, he ran down the passage but he couldn't find a bathroom anywhere. He went into her room and stood very still among her things the unmade bed the mirror on the wall shoes lying discarded stockings cigarettes and on her dressing-table a white enamel bowl and he remembered the water she had brought him last night and he ran back to his own room again. He washed the clothes in the bowl and scrubbed at them with the cloth. But blood is a durable quantity and isn't easily undone. His hands were hurting and the clothes were wet but when he put them on the stains were lessened and he didn't feel so utterly accused.

Then a knock at the door.

'Yes,' he said.

She said, 'Captain Mong would like to speak to you.'

'I'll come out,' he said.

He heard her walk down the passage. He looked at himself in the mirror. Then he followed her. The day was clear. Now the plaza was silent and deserted except for these two tiny figures at the one edge of it near the car. He went to them.

The policeman was standing facing the other way. He turned around slowly. His uniform was clean and immaculate and he was somehow transformed by it so that he was not immediately familiar. He held out his hand to the minister and the minister took it in his and as the two men shook hands they were staring with intent at each other. Then they let go and stood there. But the minister continued to stare. It was a face he had seen yesterday in a washroom mirror and hadn't thought about again. The mouth swollen redly like some edible fruit, the mole in the centre of the forehead.

9

He followed the policeman across the cracked plane of concrete towards where he didn't want to go. They passed the red
motorbike he had also seen yesterday and went past the sandbags and inside. Through an office with a counter and a
pimply boy sitting behind it through a door and into another
office. A desk and a filing cabinet and yellowed blinds on the
window and a bowl in which a goldfish was swimming. A
noticeboard filled with memos and papers and a picture of
Jesus on the wall.

The two men sat opposite each other with the surface of the
desk between them. The Captain had a white pad in front of
him and a ball-point pen in his hand. The minister had
nothing. He sat very upright in the chair with his body angled
slightly away from the Captain, fingers held together in his
lap.

He told the policeman what had happened. He started from
the time he had arrived in the town and recounted events
simply, unhurried. He spoke in a low, flat voice. The policeman looked from him to the page and only his hand was
moving. He wrote quickly. The man saw he had a neat and
tiny writing and that he pressed down hard on the page. When
he bent his head his parting was visible like a clean line ruled
down his scalp. He saw these things as he sat there. Then at
some point his eyes moved sideways and on the noticeboard
behind the Captain's shoulder there was a photograph of his
own face looking out. He stopped speaking.

The Captain looked up at him. He started speaking again.
The Captain's hand moved as it wrote. The man told him

about stopping at the café, about asking directions at the white church. When he told about the man who had showed him the way the pen stopped moving on the page. The policeman was looking at him.

'You took him in your car?'

'Yes.'

'Why did you do that?'

'He said he would show me where to go.'

The policeman pressed the mole on his forehead as though he was activating a button.

'Did he tell you his name?'

'He said his name was Valentine.'

On another white pad that was lying near his elbow the policeman printed VALENTINE and underlined it.

'What is the car registration?'

The minister looked at him.

'The number-plate number,' he said.

'I don't know.'

'It's your car.'

'I can't remember the number.'

The policeman bent down over the page. The pen scratched and scratched on the pad. Then he finished and sat upright and blew on the ink to dry it. His face was petulant and pretty, a cross between a girl and a horse. He turned the form around and held out the pen. 'Read through and sign it,' he said. He went out.

The minister got up and ran around the desk. He tore his face from the wall. When the Captain came back he was sitting again and the photograph was crumpled in his pocket. He had signed his new name to the statement he had given and was sitting there, looking at it.

10

They worked by the light of a single bulb that hung down from the roof on a length of flex. They were in a shed that adjoined the house. There was Valentine and Small. They were brothers.

They broke open the boxes and dumped their contents on the floor. Books, papers, documents, a few household objects. Ornaments. They rummaged through everything with their hands, holding things, weighing them, deciding. What they could sell or use they threw into a pile in the middle of the floor and the rest they threw into the corner to be burned.

This was the way that they worked.

Till Small picked up the cassock.

'*Wat's die?*' he said.

Valentine took it from him. 'It's mine,' he said.

'It's a dress,' Small said. And they laughed.

Valentine sat apart in a corner of the room. He held the cassock on his lap.

'Look at this.'

A shirt.

One of the boxes had letters in it. They opened some of the letters and Valentine read them aloud. But they soon got bored with this and the letters were thrown into the corner. In another box there was an identity document with a photograph of the minister on it. The photograph was grainy and smudged but they pored intently over it as if it held a clue to their future.

'Is that him?' Small said.

'*Ja,*' said Valentine. He lost interest abruptly and threw the document into the corner. He turned back to the mound on the floor.

Then Small whistled. 'Look,' he said. 'What is this?' He looked at Valentine.

'I don't know,' he said. 'I never saw the man before. Maybe his nose was bleeding.'

Small laughed shrilly. '*Ja,* maybe,' he said.

They looked at the minister's clothes. There was a great deal of blood on them.

'No,' said Valentine. 'Throw them away.'

'*Ja,*' said Small. 'Throw away.'

The clothes were thrown into the corner.

They rolled a joint and passed it between them, squatting together on the floor. Then Small had a bottle in a brown paper bag and this was also handed round. By this time they were happy.

'*Trek aan jou rok,*' Small said.

Valentine pulled on the robe. The effect in that tiny room was startling. His brother looked in silence at him.

He walked in his mantle. When he came to the door he raised his hands and turned and something fell out of the sleeve. It fluttered to the ground and lay there. He picked it up. Then he made a soft sound with his mouth.

'What is it?' Small said. He came over. They looked at it together.

It was the blue flower that the man had taken off the vine in the quarry and worn afterwards in his hair. By now it was wilted and limp.

'It looks like those ones,' said Small.

Valentine turned the flower around carefully in his palm. He looked at it from all angles. He held it to his nose and smelled it.

'Don't you think, Valentine? Don't you think it looks like those ones?'

Small took the flower from Valentine. He also smelled it and looked at it.

'It's the same,' he said.

'I don't know,' Valentine said.

'Maybe he brought it with him.'

'Who?'

'*Die man.*'

There was a silence.

'Do you think he was there?' Small said.

'Why will he go there?'

'I don't know why.'

Valentine took off the cassock. He hung it over a chair. He looked around at the room, at the objects strewn on the concrete floor. Small stood watching him.

They continued to drink as they walked. There was an air of jollity to their outing. Small ran ahead of Valentine and stopped and waited for him. Valentine was drinking. When he had finished the bottle he threw it and it burst softly off in the darkness. They walked on. The night was soft with a peppering of stars and though Valentine was carrying a torch he didn't switch it on. They knew the path they were walking. As they got closer they grew gradually quieter until they were trudging in silence.

They crossed the dirt road and in the cool dark their feet stirred up the smell of dust. Then they walked across the gravel. In the blueness the quarry was black, an absence in the surface of the world. It looked like a lake. They stood at the edge of the drop and looked down but they could see nothing below. Warm air passed up over them.

Valentine switched on the torch as they started to go down. They followed a route that was familiar. When they came to the bottom Valentine went through a narrow defile and came to the bank of green plants that the man had walked down yesterday, thinking that they were weeds. But they weren't weeds. They were the garden that Small and Valentine had planted.

'*Is daai 'n* footprint?' Small said.

Valentine didn't answer. He knelt there, thinking. Then he got up and went back through the defile and up to the vine that grew across the cliff. He had the wilted blue flower that had fallen out of his sleeve and he held it up and stood there, comparing.

'Is it the same?'

Valentine thought. 'I don't know,' he said. He dropped the flower and spat.

They searched the bottom of the quarry, shining the light into crevices and hollows. They couldn't see any sign of disturbance. They climbed back up out of the quarry.

'Who is that man?' Small said.

'I don't know who he is.'

'Do you think he was here?'

'Why will he come here?'

'I don't know why he will come here. I'm asking do you think he was here?'

'I don't know,' said Valentine.

The sky behind them was starting to lighten as they walked back slowly to the town. When they got there the sun was already coming up. There were people in the streets. They walked to the house across a vacant lot strewn with pieces of zinc and wire and the discarded innards of engines. They opened a padlocked door and came into the shed where the minister's belongings were. They looked at them.

'*Gaan ons nog rook?*' said Small.

'No. I must sleep.'

'*Kom ons maak nog 'n ding, man.*'

'No,' said Valentine. 'I want to sleep.'

He went. Small stayed behind. He sat in the corner with the cassock in his lap and he rubbed the cloth between his fingers.

It had a sensual texture that his life did not and its smoothness was strange and consoling. He sat there, rubbing. His eyes were closed. The lamp was still burning although the sun had come up and it was light in the room.

11

She lay in the bed and watched while the policeman got dressed. Naked, his body seemed fatter and looser than it did when he was clothed. He didn't look at her.

She said, 'Why don't you stay?'

'I have to meet somebody,' he said.

'Who?'

'Somebody.'

Only when he was dressed did the policeman put on his gun. He was altered, not altogether human. He went to the door. He opened it a crack and looked down the darkened passage to the closed door of the minister. He couldn't see any movement.

'He's asleep,' she said. 'Long ago.'

He went out, closing the door. He didn't kiss her or say goodbye. Those were things he never did. She could hear him going down the passage and out the front door. Then the quick footsteps fading on the plaza. She lay there a long time in the bed, her hands idly tweaking the sheets, looking around her in the room. Her clothes lying loose on the floor. A dog-eared bible on the table. A wooden crucifix on the wall. All the old symbols had died for her a long long time ago. She got out of the bed and wandered aimlessly for a bit before sitting on a chair in front of the dressing-table and looking at her body in the mirror. She held her breasts up in her hands and pointed them and let them drop again. Sat there, looking. She knew that something had to change.

12

In the veld at the edge of the township there was a ditch with brown reeds growing in it and a worn plank laid across. At night it was very dark here. The policeman came down the slope cursing, his feet snagging and sliding in holes.

The other man was waiting already. When the policeman came close he rose out of the ditch like an assassin and the two of them moved away together. They huddled head-to-head in the dark and spoke in sibilant whispers. They didn't talk for long. Then something glinted as it changed hands between them and coins splashed softly in a pocket. Then the man who had been waiting walked quickly up the slope towards the lights of the township. His figure ballooned in silhouette and went. The policeman waited at the edge of the ditch and looked around and looked up at the sky. Then he also headed back up the slope towards the township, going a different way to the other man.

13

On the night before his first sermon he borrowed a bible from the woman. He sat at the desk in the room with the crucifix hanging on the wall over him and he read certain pages in the book. He had a piece of loose paper and he made notes on it, writing in pencil. His writing was disconnected and rapid, slanting in contrary directions, and he covered the page with words. Another page, and another. Towards dawn he appeared to be satisfied and he squared the pages on the desk and placed the bible on them. He fell asleep on top of the covers without taking off his boots.

He woke late in the day to the sound of children playing outside. He got up and went down the passage to the kitchen. The woman was sitting at the table with a magazine opened in front of her and she looked up at him in alarm. The silence and the suddenness of him. His feet made no sound on the floor.

'I want to see the church,' he said.

'Tonight...'

'Before tonight,' he said.

She went to her room and came back with a key on a chain. He walked behind her. She led the way across the plaza to the church. At the far end of the concrete near the sandbags the policeman was squatting at his motorbike with a tin of polish and a cloth in his hand. He stopped working and watched them through the wheel with a canny and covert attention.

The doors were massive and wooden, mounted on iron hinges, and people had scratched their names into them. She pushed the key in and turned it. The doors cracked down the middle and yawned and they went through into the church.

It was small and dirty inside. The floor was bare earth. There was an altar of sorts at the front and a few rows of chairs and a collection box stood at the door. He walked down the nave. There were candles standing here and there in saucers. Holes in the bricks all around, pigeons roosting in the rafters overhead, pigeon shit streaked on the walls. He walked to the front and stood for a while and then he walked back to where she was waiting.

'All right,' he said. 'We can go.'

They closed the doors behind them. The policeman was standing behind his motorbike and he watched them as they walked back to the house. She said, 'Do you like to give sermons?'

'No,' he said.

He borrowed a bucket from her. In the late afternoon he walked to the communal tap and filled it and walked back. On his return he came past the red motorbike in the plaza and the Captain was lying on the concrete.

He got up. Smiling.

'First service, *Dominee*,' he said.

'Yes,' he said. 'Yes.'

The policeman was shirtless and his nipples were like purple medallions on a chest smeared with oil and with sweat. The minister looked away. The Captain came closer, wiping his hands over and over on a cloth.

'I have a lead,' he said.

The man blinked, confused. 'Oh, yes,' he said.

'With your car. With your case.'

'My case,' he said. 'Yes.'

'I'll be making an arrest soon.'

'Yes,' the man said. He stood.

Then there was a silence in the plaza and the policeman was wiping and wiping.

'I have to go,' the man said.

'Good luck with your service,' said the Captain.

He walked across to the house with the policeman's eyes like a drill-bit in his back. He went in and down to his room. He stripped naked in front of the mirror. He washed his face and shaved and then washed the rest of his body, the water cold as metal on his skin, and when he had finished he walked to the window and looked out but the policeman had gone.

14

There were twenty or thirty people in the church. They were mostly fishermen or their wives and families, the scarred and hardened people who went to sea on the boats in the bay. They were taciturn and wary. He had stood outside, watching them go in, and they had watched him in turn.

Now he went in and walked to the front of the church. He stood there a moment, looking at them. The candles placed in saucers here and there made a flickering yellow light by which he could see the faces, the hands. He carried the bible. He had no cassock and he wore the same clothes in which he had arrived, marked still with faint stains of blood. He was trembling slightly.

He started to speak. His voice was soft and they couldn't hear him. He stopped. He coughed and swallowed and wiped his palms on his shirt and looked at them and started again.

They listened. He told them that the world was a prison, that they were all prisoners in it. He told them that they could escape the prison of the world and that there was freedom beyond it and as he spoke upon his theme a sort of inspiration touched him. He spoke quietly, distinctly, but a faint grey light was glimmering on his forehead and on the backs of his hands and the faces too seemed to take on this light so that the church was lambent with its glow. He told them about freedom and the meaning of death and then he stopped speaking and stood there.

'That's all,' he said. 'Let's pray.'

The next week there were forty people there for the service and the week after that almost sixty. They could not all fit in and they jammed up the doorway and peered in through the holes in the bricks.

15

It was a huge bonfire and it had been burning for an hour in the middle of the vacant lot next to the house. There was a white heat at its centre. They had thrown into it the minister's letters, his identity book and the other things they couldn't use. Valentine had picked up the minister's clothes and he was about to consign these too to the flames when three policemen appeared suddenly out of the darkness. They had approached quite silently. One of them had his gun drawn. They were all in uniform and the light of the fire made their buttons shine redly like eyes. Small and Valentine stood staring at them and time changed shape as it does in instants of extremity.

Valentine was wearing the cassock. He had taken to wearing it lately at night or while he was in the house. It billowed around him as he walked and he felt that it somehow enlarged him. He dropped what he was holding. Now he leaped in the airy black garment and by the time he knew he had moved he had passed through the centre of the fire and was on the other side running.

Small was behind him. His feet were light and frantic and he emitted a high, keening scream. Valentine had heard a rabbit scream once with a cry not unlike this cry. He ducked to one side, as much to escape his brother as the pursuers of them both. He ran through the grass and there were rocks and holes in the ground and once he fell on a piece of twisted metal but he was up before he knew he had fallen. He ran. Though the fire was far behind him it cast long flickering shadows and the outlines of men in motion were around him and he ran without destination.

There was a log, a fence. He jumped. He landed on his feet and stumbled and ran on. Now he heard oaths from somewhere, and shouting. There was a shot. He was on ground that sloped away gently and he ran down, following the slope. He could hear feet behind him and the sound of breath and he knew that he couldn't get away. He stopped and turned. He held up his hands although it was dark and they couldn't be seen. 'It's me,' he said. 'Here. It's me.'

His hands were cuffed behind him. He walked back slowly with the policeman holding his arms. His cassock ballooned around him. It had holes burned in it from when he had jumped through the fire. When they got back Captain Mong was standing there, waiting. He looked bored. He glanced at Valentine and turned away, sucking on his moustache.

The other policemen came back. They were panting. Small wasn't with them.

'Where's he?'

'*Ek weet nie, Kaptein.* He got away.'

'Where's he?' the Captain said to Valentine.

'I don't know,' Valentine said.

'We'll get him later. Let's take this one down to the station.'

The plaza wasn't far. They made him walk. Two of them stayed behind to go through the house and Captain Mong came walking behind him.

'What's your name?' he said.

'Valentine.'

'Valentine who?'

'Valentine April.'

'Valentine April,' Captain Mong said.

'What do you want with me, Captain?'

'I don't know,' Captain Mong said. 'Maybe you stole some things out of a car.'

'I don't steal,' said Valentine.

'Nice dress,' Captain Mong said.

They came to the police-station. Inside there was a cell made out of steel with a concrete floor. They locked Valentine in it. There was a bed against one wall and a high barred window and a toilet in the corner with no seat. The cell was painted green and over the years people had scratched their names into it and the dates when they had been there.

Then Valentine was alone.

Then Captain Mong came back. He was carrying the clothes that the minister had been wearing, with the blood-stains on them.

'What's this?'

'Captain?'

'What's this?'

Valentine looked at the blood. 'I don't know, Captain,' he said.

Then Valentine was alone again for the rest of the night. He slept for a few hours on the bed, then got up and walked around. There was a light on in the corridor that shone into the cell. He shat and stood leaning against the door for a while and went back to bed and slept again. When he woke up it was day already and a shaft of sunlight was coming in through the window. The shaft moved slowly along as time went by and he could hear the sounds of voices coming in from the plaza outside. He could hear feet walking past.

16

Captain Mong outside the door in the sunlight. Smoking a cigarette with his eyes slitted, one hand hooked into his belt. When the minister came to the door he tossed a black bundle to him and said from the corner of his mouth:

'That it?'

The minister unfolded the cassock. He held it up, looking at it.

'Yes.'

'Come with me.'

He folded the cassock over his arm and followed the policeman across the plaza. They went in past the sandbags and the red motorbike and down a passage round a corner to a door. The door had bars in it that cut the world into vertical strips and in the square room on the far side was a man, lying on the bed.

Captain Mong kicked the door with his boot. '*Kom hier, doos,*' he said.

Valentine came to the door.

'That him?' Captain Mong said.

'Yes.'

'*Ag,* give me a cigarette, Captain.'

The Captain gave him a cigarette. He lit it for him through the bars.

'Remember this man?' he said.

'What man?' Valentine said.

'This one.'

The two men looked at each other through the intervening iron. The face of one was scarified with scars and the face of the other was smooth.

'I did nothing,' Valentine said.

'Come on.'

'A few clothes. It's nothing.'

'Come,' Captain Mong said.

The minister turned and walked after the policeman. Valentine called down the passage.

'I saw the flower,' he said.

In Captain Mong's office the goldfish was swimming in its bowl. There was a newspaper open on the desk with a crossword half finished in it. There was a large pile of clothes on the floor.

'Those them?' Captain Mong said.

'Yes,' he said. 'Yes.'

'You can have them back. Just sign this form for me.'

'How did you find him?'

The policeman pulled his ear. 'I hear things,' he said. 'I know things.'

The minister signed the form. He knelt down by the clothes and started arranging them neatly. There was a silence for a while, then he said:

'What happens now?'

'To who?'

'To him.'

The policeman shrugged. 'He stays here. There's a circuit court that comes every few months. He can wait till the next one.'

'Yes,' he said.

There were too many clothes to be carried across in one trip. The policeman made no offer to help him. The man took an armload of clothes and went out and across the plaza to the house. When he came back the Captain was sitting behind the desk, staring at the crossword. He glanced up idly.

'Those yours?' he said.

He was pointing to the blood-stained clothes that the minister had been wearing.

The man looked at them. 'No,' he said.

'No,' the Captain said. 'They weren't with your things. I just thought.'

He went on with his crossword.

The man made another trip. Out of the station, across the plaza to the house. When he came back the Captain had filled in two words in the puzzle. He said, 'Do I know you?'

He stopped. 'What do you mean?'

The Captain looked up. 'Do I know you? From before you came here.'

'No,' the man said.

'Oh.' The Captain looked down. 'It feels like I saw you before.'

He took another armload of clothes. He went and came back again. He gathered up the last load and was about to go out. The Captain tapped his teeth with a pencil.

'"The evil leader is after flesh,"' he said, '"and there's no escape."'

There was silence for a moment.

'Fate,' said the man.

He went out.

17

Captain Mong finished the crossword. He folded up the paper and threw it into the bin behind him. Then he sat for a time at his desk staring ahead at nothing, sucking on his moustache.

It was a hot, clear day. Sunlight slanted into the office in long transverse beams and motes of dust were visible going past. He got up. He went to the cupboard that stood against one wall and opened it. He took out a box and took from it a pinch of colourless flakes which he sprinkled on the water in the bowl. The goldfish rose hungrily to eat.

He put away the fish-food and from the same cupboard he removed a black plastic bag with something wadded inside it. He held it for a moment meditatively. Then he closed the cupboard and went out of the office, closing that door behind him. He was a meticulous man.

On the way he leaned into a room and gave a peremptory grunt. Two black policemen came out and followed him. Their uniforms and expressions were identical. All three of them went down the passage to the cell. Captain Mong unlocked it and they went inside and closed that door behind them too.

Valentine stood up when he saw them. He had been lying on the bed with his hands behind his head, looking up at the roof. His shoes were on the floor. He moved away to a corner, his eyes fixed on the three men and an expression on his face of increasing unease, as if a thought was troubling his mind.

'I think...' he said. 'I think...'

But he didn't finish.

'Valentine April,' said the Captain. His tone was amused and remote.

He sat on the edge of the bed. The two black policemen stayed standing, formal and correct, on either side of the door. The light that came in through the window was diffused by the grid of metal and fell in daubs and slivers on the floor, the walls.

'It's funny in here,' said the Captain. 'It's funny to be in this room.'

Valentine said nothing.

'The world doesn't look normal from in here. When you try to look out, the bars, they make things look funny.'

Valentine was in the corner now, his back pressed to the wall.

'You don't want to be in here.'

'No,' Valentine said.

'Me also, I don't want you in here. I have to watch you, give you food. You give me trouble.'

Valentine didn't move. Only his eyes were blinking.

'Also you tell me lies. You tell me you're not a thief. You say you don't know where the blood on your clothes came from. You say you don't know where your brother is hiding.'

'I don't know,' Valentine said, his voice rising shrilly now. 'But I don't know.'

'Valentine April,' said the Captain musingly. 'Valentine, Valentine April.'

He was shaking his head. Smiling tenderly as an uncle, he opened the black plastic bag that he had taken from his cupboard. He took out a handful of leaves and ran his fingers gently through them. They released a scent that was vivid and distinct in the room. He looked into Valentine's eyes.

'And this, Valentine. And this.'

'I don't know,' Valentine said.

'Maybe you like this room. Maybe you want to stay in this room.'

'No,' Valentine said.

'Where do you grow this?'

'I don't grow it.'

'It was picked two, three days ago.'

'Maybe.'

'Where does it come from?'

'I don't know.'

Captain Mong turned to the policemen. He made a gesture. One of the men went out. The other one waited at the door, rolling up his sleeves.

Captain Mong glanced around idly. He had that amused, disdainful look again. 'Have you written your name on the wall yet?' he said.

'No.'

'But you must. It's a *tradition*.'

'Where's he gone?'

'He'll come back.'

The policeman came in. He had an assortment of things that he threw down on the floor. It was hard to make them out but there was what appeared to be a tube and a sack of some rubbery material. There was something made out of metal.

'Where are you going?'

Captain Mong turned at the door. 'If you remember where your garden is, maybe I'll come back.'

'But I –' Valentine said.

Captain Mong went out and back to his office. He got a rag and a tin of polish and went out again and into the plaza. The sentry greeted him and he called back cheerily. The red motorbike stood beyond the wall of sandbags. It was large and fat and dramatic. He took off his shirt and set to work with the rag, rubbing the polish into the planes of steel until his face was uncovered in them. His back, his shoulders hurt.

Later his sister came to visit. She drove up in her yellow Triumph and parked. They sat in the sun on the rampart of sandbags and drank beer which she had brought with her. Her name was Miems. She was married to the minister of the white church in the town and she was fond of her brother.

She looked across the plaza to the church. 'They've got a new minister,' she said.

'How do you know?'

'He stopped to ask me the way.'

'Oh, *ja*,' he said. 'This beer is warm.'

She kissed him goodbye. 'Come and visit,' she said.

'*Ja*.'

'*Liefie*,' she called. '*Kom, liefie.*'

She went nowhere without her white dog.

He stood at the edge of the plaza and waved as her car disappeared. Then there was only dust and the plaza was empty and immense. His motorbike stood tilted to one side, giving off light like a sun. Behind his eyes he felt the shimmer of a headache. He started to put on his shirt.

'Captain!'

He turned. It was one of the policemen he had left in the cell, his broad face shiny with sweat. He was smiling. As he looked at him Captain Mong tasted something in his mouth that had a faintly sourish flavour to it.

'He remembered.'

18

Small spent the night lying face-down in a ditch. He emerged when it was light again, his arms wrapped around himself, trembling. He wandered through the streets in which other people were also afoot, looking for something that might console him. He went near to the house once but there was a policeman sittng on the back step smoking and he walked hastily away.

Later he ran into Harry. Harry worked with them sometimes. He was a large man with a black eye-patch and fingers that were thickened with rings. He had heard the news, he told Small. 'Everybody heard.'

'Where's Valentine?' Small said.

'They got him.'

'The *boere*?'

'*Ja*. They took him down to the station.'

Small sat down on the kerb to consider this news. He held his head in his hands.

They were at the side of a road. The road was at the edge of the township. Behind them there were houses in geometrical rows and before them the veld stretched away. The sun came vertically down.

'*Wat moet ons nou maak?*'

Harry smirked. '*Ek weet nie wat jy moet maak nie.* Me, I'm not doing anything.'

Small started to cry. He wiped his nose on his sleeve.

'*Jy's vol blare.*'

He picked at the leaves on his shirt. He stopped crying and Harry sat down next to him. They stared out over the grass.

'Is it because of the car?'

'I think it is.'

They sat in the sun. Time passed.

'What about the *boom*?' said Harry.

'In the house?'

'No, man. The other place.'

Small thought.

'Do you think he will tell them?'

'I don't know.'

'Why will he tell them?'

'I don't know.'

A wagon came past in the road. A horse was in the traces, its head down. An old man sat on the wagon with a frayed whip in his hand. He looked at them as he went past. There was dust.

'It's hot,' Small said.

'*Kom ons gaan kry 'n drankie.*'

They went to a room nearby. It was cool inside and there were wooden tables and faded prints on the wall. They drank beer. Harry paid.

'Do you think he will say about the *dagga*?'

'*Ek weet nie*. What do you think?'

'Why will he say?'

Harry lifted one fist significantly and brought it down on the table. Both of them looked at the fist.

'No,' Small said.

They drank more.

'Maybe we must go there.'

Harry smirked again. 'And do what?'

'Pull it up. Throw it away.'

'It's got nothing to do with me,' Harry said.

Small set out for the quarry in the mid-afternoon. His shadow stretched out in front of him. He had never gone there in daylight before and he kept looking furtively behind him. But nobody else was around and the landscape lay passive in the sun. Even the road was untravelled.

At this hour there was still light in the quarry. One side of
it was in shadow but across the rock face on the other side the
sun burned yellow and steady and the ground was hot to the
touch. He went down by the usual path and at first he walked
in the light but by the time he had descended halfway he was
overtaken by shadow and it was blue and cool at the bottom.
The gnarled trees crouched in their attitudes of stasis and the
rocks lay inert and watchful.

Small spoke to himself and answered.

'What smells like that?'

'Like what?'

'Can't you smell something?'

'No, man. Let's hurry.'

He went through the defile to the bank of weeds. The plants
were green and prolific. He knelt down and started uprooting
them in handfuls, undoing the work that they'd done. He
threw them down in a pile on the ground that gradually
mounted and swelled.

'Will Valentine mind?' he said to himself.

'No,' he said. 'He'll be proud.'

Then the bank was clear. The plants lay in a matted mass,
wilting slowly in the air. He stood there a moment looking
down at the bare soil, panting and sweating from his labour.
His hands were dirty with earth.

'What are we going to put them in?'

'We can't leave them here.'

'Isn't there a bag or a packet or something?'

'Look around. Maybe there's something lying around.'

Small went back through the defile into the garden on the
other side. The vine grew up along the cliff-face with its
burden of intermittent flowers. They gave off a scent. But
there was another smell on the air that mingled with the scent
of the flowers and it was redolent of decay and putrefaction
and it was sourceless, this smell. He walked around a little.

Then he came to the hole.

He stood at the edge, looking down. There was a pyramid of rocks. Nothing else could be seen but there was a stench on the air and flies were thickly clustered like grapes.

'What is it?'

'I don't know what it is.'

'Let's go.'

He stood there. The shadow had reached the top of the quarry and the sky was cooling now.

Small climbed down into the hole. He stood there, helpless and looking. Then he reached out and took a stone from the pile and dropped it down heavily behind him.

'What is it?' Small said.

'I don't know what it is.'

Flies rose droning around him and the miasma of corruption was sweet. Small stood rigid, his body poised to run while he worked. He lifted the stones and dropped them. In time the truth was uncovered.

'*Jissus*. No. No. *Jissus*.'

He got out of the hole. He was sweating and his hands were shaking. He stood there, staring down. Then he got back into the hole and continued with what he was doing. He picked up the rocks and he dropped them.

An arm, a shoulder were apparent.

'I'm going to be sick,' Small said.

He went faster and faster. Then he stopped. He leaned against the side of the hole and covered his face with his hand.

A pebble hit Small on the arm. He looked up. It was close to dusk now and the sky was dark blue in colour but it was still possible to see in outline against it the forms of three men looking down. They were at the top of the quarry. It was Captain Mong and two others. They were standing very still and in their uniforms and caps they were like models of men. They stood there, looking, not moving.

19

In the night there are torches moving and voices calling out in the dark. In the open gravel area at the top of the quarry there are cars parked with their headlights shining and radios playing and men standing waiting and there are men at the bottom of the quarry, moving with lights among the trees and the boulders. Most of the torches are around the hole in the ground. There are people in the hole, picking amongst the rocks, shouting out to each other. Photographs are taken. Yellow tape is tied.

At some point a stretcher is carried down the side of the quarry and assembled at the bottom. Then men in plastic gloves with cloths tied over their mouths and noses lift the white form from the base of the hole and raise it hand over hand and lay it down on the stretcher. It is faceless, sexless, no longer human. It's covered with a blanket. Then two men take the stretcher and ascend with it, stopping every little while to rest. They come to the summit in time.

The body is placed in the back of a van and the van is driven away.

Some of the men stay behind.

When dawn breaks everybody has gone except for a solitary policeman who loiters at the bottom of the quarry. He is tired and bored and he slouches against a rock with his cap pushed back on his head. He yawns and scratches himself and goes wandering around again, whistling to himself.

He stops for a while at the edge of the hole and peers into it. Rocks lie tumbled at the bottom and a few flies buzz aimlessly around. Something has happened here but he doesn't know what and he doesn't particularly care. He has been left to keep watch.

20

In the café in the town the proprietor leaned on his dirty fridge while he counted change into the till. Late afternoon sun came in through the door. There were people standing at the counter.

'In the quarry?'

'That's what I heard.'

'A white man?'

'That's what I heard.'

'I heard a black woman.'

'And they found him there? Burying it?'

'Digging it up.'

'Why would they dig it up?'

'It's what I heard.'

There was shuffling and shaking of heads. Someone else came into the shop.

'Why did they kill her?'

'For money.'

'How many of them?'

'Two.'

'Four.'

'Five,' the proprietor said gravely.

'Was it a white that they killed?'

'These people. Jesus. These people.'

'They should let them know how it feels.'

21

He stood behind the curtain in his room and watched the policeman at his bike. Captain Mong was shirtless again. He had his back to the man. He was crouched down on the concrete, a soiled cloth in his hand, polishing. He worked with small violent motions, sweat oozing out of him like wax.

Then he stopped very suddenly, as if an idea had come to him. At first he sat very still. He leaned forward and breathed on the steel and brought the cloth up and rubbed where he had breathed. He stood slowly and turned. He stayed there quite still with his arms at his sides, looking across the concrete to the house.

The man moved back behind the curtain with his spine to the wall. He was rigid and shivering and his eyes were opened wide. He stood like this without stirring. There was no sound from outside.

After a while he knelt down at the window and lifted up the bottom of the curtain. The policeman was polishing again. He was crouched as before with his back to the man, his hand moving in those small violent circles.

22

A mattress had been thrown down on the floor and Small sat on it, cross-legged, waiting. It was late afternoon. He got up and went to the door and looked out through the bars into the passage. He couldn't see anything. He came back and sat down on the mattress again.

He spoke to himself and he answered.

'They taking a long time with him.'

'Same as with me, *broer.*'

'Is it the same?'

'It's the same, man.'

Then silence. Small lay back on the mattress. A fly was buzzing near the ceiling somewhere and the sound was thin and persistent. Small pulled at his hands and touched twice at his hair.

'It's not the same,' he said.

There were footsteps in the passage outside. Then a jangling of keys. Small sat up on the bed and he was as stiff as an idol. The door opened and Valentine came in and the door closed behind him again. The footsteps, the metal keys receded.

Valentine stood there. He was looking down at the floor. Then he went to the edge of the bed and sat down. His hands hung down between his knees.

Small took one of Valentine's hands. Valentine pulled it away. 'Don't do that,' he said.

In appearance the two brothers didn't look like each other beyond the eroded blue tattoos on their arms. Small was a tiny man with a hairless freckled body and a high voice that came out of his nose. He moved in an agitated way. Valentine was the elder by almost ten years and his complexion and his manner were darker. Pale scars ran across one cheek but otherwise his surface was intact.

'Did you tell them?'

'*Ja,* I told them.'

'What?'

'I told them everything that happened.'

Valentine lay back on the bed with one arm across his face. His feet were still on the floor.

Small also lay down.

The fly was buzzing near the ceiling still, its drone like a voice without words.

Small started to cry. His sobs were high-pitched and muffled with a thin edge of hysteria to them. He cried like a child. Valentine turned his head to look at him, then rolled his head the other way.

Small stopped crying. 'Who is he?' he said.

'Who?'

'That man, that minister man.'

Valentine sat up. 'He's not a minister,' he said.

23

He stood at the front of the church and waited for the congregation to file out. He was wearing the black robe with the holes burned into it and he had a bible in one hand and he stood next to the altar, waiting for the church to be empty.

Then everybody had gone except for a single figure near the door. It was dark in that corner and only when he stirred and stepped forward could the minister see who it was. He looked at the policeman.

'How long were you watching?' he said.

'Ten minutes or so.'

He nodded. The church was lit with candles. He moved from one to the other, blowing them out as he went. Thin trails of smoke rose up behind him. When he came to the last one he picked it up and walked with it towards the policeman. His face was lit in orange from below.

'Did you want to talk to me?' he said.

The policeman nodded. '*Ja,*' he said. 'I've got something to ask you.'

They stood there for a long moment. The minister watched the face of the policeman. Then he blew out the candle and set it aside on a chair.

The policeman said: 'I've got a body in my care. It must be buried.'

'Yes?'

'Will you do it?'

'Oh,' the man said. 'Yes. Is that all?'

'*Ja,* that's all.'

They continued to stand without moving. They were very

close to each other and the man could feel the breath, the heat of the policeman. He moved a little away.

They went out of the church together. He closed and locked the wooden doors behind them. The red motorbike was standing in the centre of the plaza, burning silver in the moonlight, and both of them stood staring at its shape.

The silence went on too long and neither of them had moved.

The policeman said, 'Do you want to go for a ride?'

They walked towards the motorbike in tandem, their heels striking simultaneously on the concrete.

'Where are we going to?'

'Just for a ride.'

He waited for Captain Mong to get on. He turned the key and kicked down and it started.

He got on to the seat behind him. He had his bible down the front of his shirt. He put his arms around the policeman and pressed his chest to his spine and enclosed in this unlikely embrace the two men moved forward together. The bike went across the plaza and out at the southern end and they rode without speaking through the dark streets, between the houses.

They came to the dirt road that went out of the township. They rode south. The white town rose in front of them and they passed through it and went on. Then they were on the road that had brought him to the town. Objects approached at speed and smeared back past them and away and the road rushed below them like a river.

They came to the quarry. They went past it but the policeman slowed almost immediately and made a sweeping turn in the road. The sky was clear, untouched by cloud, and starred with static points of light. A meteor fell flaming and was gone.

The acre of gravel looked metallic in the night. They rode lightly across it and parked. In the silence that followed the minister looked around. There was the termite hill and the bunches of scrub and the dark waiting brink of the hole.

They got off the bike. The minister's hands felt stiffened with cold. His skin was tingling and glowing. He walked away, his feet crunching softly on the gravel, and came to the edge of the quarry. He stood there, looking down.

Captain Mong came up next to him. Their breath was vaporous on the air. There was silence.

A cold wind blew in from the west, carrying the smell of the sea. A creature called out somewhere with a thin, plaintive cry. A night animal of some kind, predator or prey. The policeman shifted slightly on his feet.

'When I first heard your name,' he said, 'I was expecting somebody else.'

The minister watched him and waited. It was a time before the policeman spoke again.

'I was expecting a coloured man.'

The minister smiled. 'We all are. By now. In this country.'

'No,' said the policeman. 'We're white.'

There was a silence again. The policeman put his hands in his pockets. He looked acutely uncomfortable. He was staring down into the depths of the quarry where indeterminate shapes were conjoined.

'Did you hear what happened here?' he said.

The minister ran his tongue around his lips. 'Everybody heard,' he said.

'But I got them.'

'I heard that too.'

'*Dominee*,' he said. 'They're saying things about you.'

The minister crouched down. He picked up a handful of gravel and ran it through his fingers. When there was one pebble left he held out his hand and he dropped it. It fell swiftly below them without sound.

'I'm a man of God.'

'I know that, *Dominee*. I believe you.'

They looked at each other. Somewhere beyond the horizon there was a distant throbbing of lightning and each of them saw the face of the other, momentary and blanched. The silence went on and went on. The minister dropped his eyes.

'And this is the body you want buried?'

'*Ja*,' said Captain Mong. 'It's the one. Do you mind?'

'No,' he said. 'It's my job.'

From the quarry a sudden squall of bats erupted and fanned out, seared into silhouette by lightning in a pattern esoteric and exact as though exhaled by the earth. The man stood up. As if by agreement they walked back slowly together across the gravel. It was cold. They got on to the bike. They rode back together to the town. The minister held on the whole way and he could feel the policeman's heart beating under his hand.

24

The graveyard was at one edge of the township some distance away from the church. It was not like any graveyard he had ever been in before. There was only a fence to mark the edges of it and the graves were mounds of earth with wooden crosses pegged into them and names burned into the crosses and weeds grew up between the graves.

At the one end there was a man with a spade. He was sitting on a flat rock, smoking a cigarette. He watched the minister. The minister walked towards him. He was wearing the black robe again and carrying a bible.

A little way from where the man was sitting there was a mound of raw earth and stones. He went to it and at the bottom of a rectangular hole the long wooden box was lying. It was made from pine planks that fitted neatly together and he could see patterns in the wood.

The grave-digger was watching him. He could feel his eyes. He opened the bible. He looked down at it but the words on the page were opaque and meaningless and he closed the book again and stood. He started to tremble and his shoulders were shaking and he walked over to the man with the spade. He sat down on the flat rock next to him.

The man looked surprised. He was a black man with a face aged from work. He took a box of cigarettes from a pocket in his overalls and tapped one out for the minister. Then he put away the cigarettes and from another pocket he took a box of matches and lit it for him. They sat side by side on the rock in the sun and smoked and looked out on the graves.

'What's your name?' the minister said.

The black man shrugged expansively, turning his broad palms outward. It was clear that he didn't understand.

'Your name,' said the minister, and gestured.

'Jonas,' the black man said.

'Jonas,' said the minister. 'Good name.'

They sat there smoking, not talking. The sun was warm on their skin and there were sounds from the veld. When he had smoked the cigarette down the minister stubbed it out and flicked the butt away. He stood up.

'Thanks,' he said. 'Jonas.'

The other man nodded and smiled.

He walked back to the open hole in the ground and stood at the head of it and looked. The box was no different to before. He looked at it and at the earth in the hole that had been prematurely bared to the light. Then he bent down and picked up a clod and threw it down on the wood, it could have been in benediction or dismissal. He turned and walked back through the graveyard. By the time he came to the gate he could hear the sound of the spade in the ground and the noise of soil hitting wood but he didn't turn around or look.

25

He sat for most of that day in his room. The curtains were drawn and the light was dim inside and if sounds carried in they were distant and distorted, like noises made underwater.

He sat on the edge of the bed with his hands clasped and elbows resting on his knees. He didn't move. Only his eyes moved sometimes.

Later he got up. The window behind the drawn curtains was closed and the air was stale and dense. He stood for a long moment again. Only his eyes were shifting in his face but they saw nothing there in that room.

He went out and down the passage. At the end of the passage was the kitchen. The woman was sitting at the table, painting red lacquer on her nails.

It was a tiny room with grease ingrained on the walls and formica inlaid on the dressers and table-top and a strip of flypaper dangling in the corner. A single raw bulb hung down.

She looked up at him, startled.

There was silence. He was leaning forward over the table as if some support inside him had broken and he started suddenly to cry.

'What's the matter?' she said. 'What's wrong?'

His mind was filled with words but there was no syntax to them and he went out into the plaza. It was late afternoon and the shadow of the police-station stretched towards him over the concrete. The wall of sandbags was laid across his path. There was a policeman with a gun.

'I want the Captain,' he said.

The policeman pointed. 'Where they're putting up the tent.'

The minister lurched back across the plaza, in the direction that had been pointed out to him. The woman was in the doorway of the house. She was gesticulating and saying something to him, but he went on.

In the open tract of land between the township and the town there was a crowd of people gathering. They stood in groups and little clumps among the wind-burned grass. As he drew closer he saw that there were caravans parked in a circular formation and an expanse of canvas lying on the ground. The canvas was limp. There were men in overalls holding ropes in their hands. He saw all this and recognized it but it was random colours and movement to him and he passed through the commotion without interest. He was looking for the policeman.

He walked towards the caravans. He stopped. There was a cage nearby with straw inside it and a group of children taunting something through the bars. He turned around and went back. He passed two dwarves who were running hand in hand and there were feral odours on the air. Then he saw Captain Mong. One hand on his hip and his cap pushed back on his head.

The policeman waved a hand at the tent. 'Every five years or so they come.'

'Captain –'

'I can't hear you, *Dominee*.'

The crowd was cheering and calling. The men with the ropes in their hands were pulling and the canvas hung alive for a moment and then it died and descended again.

'Please,' he said. 'The trial...'

'*Ja?*'

'I have to speak to you,' he said.

'Not now, *Dominee*. All right?'

Ho took hold of the policeman's arm. His voice rose suddenly like the sound of glass being rubbed. 'It mustn't happen,' he said.

'What?'

'The trial... It... I...'

He was desperate for words.

The policeman leaned towards him and took his hand off his arm. He held the minister's hand as he spoke. He talked clearly, distinctly, each word exact:

'Not now, *Dominee*. All right?'

He let go his hand.

The man stood trembling, alert, his body enclosed by a nimbus, his mouth open to speak. Then he suddenly went slack. He was one moment full and the next moment empty, as if the contents had been scooped out of him. He was tired. The words that had been leavening in him receded now. He stood there and though there were people all around him it felt as if he stood alone on a hilltop. The sun came down whitely and there was no sound and he was alone on a hill.

He turned and walked back towards the township. When he came to the edge of the grass he stopped. The crowd was larger than before and other people were streaming out from the houses with expressions of delight on their faces. There was a surge of movement. The ropes tautened and the canvas rose up over the crowd like a kite and there were cheers and small bursts of applause and this time the tent didn't fall.

He walked away over the grass, going in the direction of the sea. He walked quickly, going at speed, and soon he left the crowded place behind. The township receded and the spires of the town and then he was stumbling through marshland.

He came in time to the sea. The water stretched away in a flat grey immensity and waves ran up on the sand. He took his shoes off and walked and he could feel the granules on his feet with a heightened and almost painful awareness and there were rocks here and there and pools in the rocks and things grew and lived in the pools. Tiny fish the colour of rust and fronds that had the texture of flesh. He walked with his shoes in his hand. The shore was desolate and cold. The sun was going down and he was a solitary traveller tonight. There was kelp and flotsam lying scattered on the sand and crabs moved like small armies dancing.

After a time he came to a headland that thrust out into the water. He walked to the end of it and sat. The headland was made of rocks, haphazard and black, and nothing grew here except mussels. There was the sound of water. Salt accreted on his skin. He sat, crouched over like an old man or a baby, as the last light went out of the sky and the stars began to flicker overhead. The darkness was strong and he couldn't see the horizon and he sat there as if waiting for something. A ship went slowly past far out in the water like a burning city floating out to sea.

When he got back to the house the woman and Captain Mong were sitting in the kitchen. There was another man with them. This man was the doctor.

They took him to his room. 'You're sick, *Dominee*,' they said. 'You must rest.'

'Yes,' he said. 'Yes.'

'You must get into bed.'

'You're not well.'

They helped him undress and he got into the bed and their faces were above him like the faces of gods and they looked down from a great height on him.

26

The dimensions of objects would not remain constant and they waxed and waned in constellations. They appeared between interstices of sleep and he experienced them as textures or as qualities of intensity and only later did they resolve themselves, sometimes quite suddenly, at other times by degrees, into a coherence that he could name: desk window chair floor wall

The woman was there too. Once she helped him to use the bedpan. He said to her

I'm sorry.

It doesn't matter, she said. She smiled at him.

It was hard to tell as he lay there whether it was day or night or what time of day or night it was. He could feel the mattress under him and he seemed always to be tangled up in the sheets but then sometimes he was not in bed at all but outside lying on the ground under the branches of a huge spreading tree Why have you brought me here he said why have you she laughed at him I didn't bring you she said you came

At other times he was in chains. He could not move his arms or legs and he raised his head to see he saw that he was not chained but was floating in a vast expanse of water that spread around him, saline and green, upholding him warmly from below fish nibbled at him and the sun went down redly over the sea and he saw that he was not after all in water but drifting through a darkness a space and it came to him that that was what nothing was the absence of shape but how can that be he said I am a shape

Then the doctor came and touched him on the forehead, the

wrists the fever is bad he said i must inject him again the doctor brought pain and after the pain he felt cooler again the room began to coagulate around him, he saw the crucifix hanging over the desk, he saw the grain in the wood. Then Captain Mong came. He sat next to the woman at the side of the bed and he touched at her with his hands. The woman went. The Captain was alone next to the bed and he tried to speak to the Captain, i have done something he said if you have done something Shh said the Captain Shhh

and then

and then he swung the bottle and the wine exploded redly like blood like blood or perhaps it was blood he had blood all over his hand i cut it on a piece of wire next to the road when i stopped but you must clean that she said

She cleaned him all over with a cloth she sat him up in the bed and wiped him under the arms the neck

It will never come off, he said

Don't talk, she said

Thank you for doing this

It's all right, she said

But it will never come off

What are you talking about, she said

She lay him back down on the bed, the cool sheets He slept and

then he rose slowly again to the surface of things and he was in the bed in the room in the house He could see the black robe hanging skewly across the back of the chair and he could see its creases, its folds It was morning and a thin wash of sunlight came in past the curtains, casting small pools of shadow, and he felt the edges of the light acutely as though they were made out of stone. Everything had a lustre and a brilliance to his eyes that he had never detected before and he looked around with a kind of awe at the shimmer and luminance of forms. He could smell odours and fragrances from close by and far and sounds penetrated his ear with a piquancy that hurt him. 'What's that?' he said. 'What's that?'

'It's music,' she said. 'That's all.'

'What music?'

'Circus music,' she said.

27

It carried over the plaza, tinny and distant, and found its way through the high barred window into the cell. The three men lifted their heads for a moment.

'What's that?' Small said.

'It's circus music,' said the lawyer. 'They're practising.'

The lawyer was a soft short man with stiff brown hair combed back and a front tooth made of gold. His hands as they shuffled papers had a nervous air to them. He wouldn't look directly at the men.

He had come into the cell shortly before. They hadn't asked for him. The door had opened and he was standing there with a striped suit on and a briefcase and with his pale face and his out-turned feet he was himself not unlike a clown.

'Who are you?' Small said.

'I'm your lawyer.'

'We didn't ask for a lawyer.'

'I've been appointed for you by the State. Your trial is coming up, gentlemen.'

He sat on the edge of the bed. His briefcase was open on his knees. He had a sheaf of papers in his hands which he kept referring to intently and his demeanour was slope-shouldered and unhappy. It was clear that he wished himself elsewhere.

'We don't want a lawyer,' said Valentine.

They were all very still in the cell.

'But you –'

'We don't want a lawyer. Get out.'

'Without a lawyer there isn't much chance –'

'Get out, I said. Get out.'

The lawyer sat rigid for a moment. Then he gathered his papers together and neatened them with his fingertips and put them into his briefcase. He closed it and got up. He looked at them and walked to the door. He knocked on it loudly and waited. His vast pinstriped back to them. When the door was opened he went out.

Small looked at Valentine. Small's face was frightened. Valentine took from his shoe what looked like a silver splinter or a blade. But it wasn't. It was a spoon. It was bright and precise in his palm. He crouched down and began to rub it against the wall. The sound it gave off was high and thin like a baby crying.

He stopped and looked up at Small.

'What are you doing?' said Small.

Valentine gestured once. 'Watch at the door,' he said.

'What are you doing?'

'What does it look like I'm doing?'

Small watched at the door. Valentine started and again the cell was filled with the thin high noise.

'What are you going to do with that?' Small said.

'I'll find something to do with it.'

Small watched him. For an instant the movement stopped and Valentine looked at his brother in the gloom with his eyes glinting dimly like a rodent's eyes. Then his hands started moving again. The spoon was outlined in a thin thread of heat and Small was very still at the door. Only Valentine's hands were moving with a separate volition like creatures he couldn't control as if by their repeated and violent agitation making up for what both of them had lost.

28

'This high it was growing. This high.'
   'They say that he –'
   'They'll say anything. To save themselves.'
   'Shame.'
   'I hope they –'
   'And they tried to blame –'
   'Do you think it'll be full?'
   'You better go early, if you go. Are you going?'
   'I'm going.'
   'It's the circus tomorrow too.'
   'The circus will come again.'
   'I don't know.'
   'I can't go. The shop –'
   'I'm going.'
   'I'm not.'
   'I'm going.'

29

The youngest of them was a child and the oldest a man of ninety. There were whole families and couples and some single people, all dressed in the smartest clothes that they had, dark suits or dresses of floral crimplene, hats and button-holes and rosettes and one of them even in medals that had been awarded to somebody else in a war.

There were too many of them. They could not all fit into the white church, which was where the court was held, there being no courthouse in the town, and they milled around on the slate outside, speaking brightly to each other, all of them edging closer to the door that was still closed but very soon would be opened.

Their eyes moving quickly.

'There. That's him.'

'Where? Where?'

'Him there. Isn't that him?'

'No. That's somebody else.'

'Where are *they*?'

Then the doors were opened. The people started to go through into the church. Some of them had never been here before and they looked around at the ordered rows of pews and the tall windows made of fragments of coloured glass and at the altar and the huge crucified figure only slightly smaller than an actual man affixed to the wall in bronzed and perpetual torment. They sat. There were policemen here and there at various points in the church. The church filled quickly. Then the doors were closed again. The policeman stood at the back and turned the latecomers away and there were many disappointed that day.

But from outside the church the top of the striped tent was visible in the distance and it was towards this that they began to go now, streaming across the uneven ground singly or hand in hand like pilgrims setting out on a journey and soon the slate was empty again.

Now those inside the church were looking around, whispering to each other. A desk and a chair had been set out at the front and a flag was hung hugely behind it. The choir was the single area as yet unoccupied and it was clear that this was to be the dock but of the accused there wasn't a sign. Nor of the minister or the policeman or of any other official.

And the heat. And the waiting. And the eyes. That audience began to grow restless.

Then the side door to the vestry opened and Captain Mong came in, followed by the two prisoners. He led them to the choir-stall and watched them sit. He unlocked the padlocks on their wrists and took the handcuffs with him. He went back to the vestry door and stood there.

The crowd watched the prisoners in the dock. How they sat. At what they were looking. The two men were very still and apart on those lonely wooden benches.

Then a voice said All Rise and another side door opened, one near the apse of the church, and the judge came in and went to the table near the altar and sat. He wore a red robe and without it he would be in no way remarkable. He was a small man with hair turned prematurely ashen and brushed straight back from his forehead. His hands were plump and freckled and he took a long time to settle at the desk. When his papers were arranged about him he looked around across the top of his glasses until his gaze fell on the prosecutor and he nodded.

30

In an office next to the vestry the man sat waiting to be called. He could hear through the wall faint intimations of what was taking place in the church. Raised voices, chairs shifting, the gavel. He coughed. It was hot in the room. He sat with his hands together, palm to palm.

Now another sound carried into the room. It was reedy and percussive and merry and came in intermediate staccato phrases. Circus music. He listened for a while. Then he got up and walked around the room.

He stopped when he came to the window. He looked out into the deserted stretch of street on which the sun was whitely pouring but his gaze seemed fastened on some vista or happening elsewhere and his lips shaped words he didn't speak. He looked down at his hands. On his finger the cut had healed by now but there was the faint brown outline of a scar and he brought it up to his mouth and touched it with the tip of his tongue. Then he lowered his hand again. He walked back to his seat but something had changed in him now and he sat differently to how he had sat before.

He wore the same clothes in which he had first come to the town and which he took off only to wash. The stains were less distinct than before but they were still there on the front of the shirt, the pants, like the outline of a continent on a map, a private marking known only to him. Sun came in the window. It fell in a yellow beam on the carpet and there were flies lying dead at the base of the glass and a clock was ticking somewhere with a soft glottal sound like somebody swallowing over and over.

At noon the court broke for an hour. Though the church was empty and the silence it gave off was immense he didn't himself leave the room and he asked for nothing to eat or drink. In the afternoon the proceedings resumed and shortly afterward the circus. Once again these separate discords were mingled in the room as if produced only for his torment. There was a quality to his waiting now of expectation, of imminence, and his chin was resting on his hand and his eyes were no longer downcast.

Then the door was opened and it was Captain Mong. 'They want you now,' he said.

'Yes,' he said. He stood up.

'Are you feeling all right?'

'Yes,' he said. 'I'm all right.'

He followed the policeman into the court. He walked to the witness box. A lectern had been set up for this purpose with an iron chair behind it. Over his clothes the man wore as always that scorched black robe and he looked more like a beggar than a preacher and there was a sound of breath from the spectators in the pews. The judge rapped once with his gavel. Yet even the judge was watchful. The man turned at the edge of the lectern and across the breadth of that sanctified space faced the eyes of the two men accused. He looked at them and then he looked down.

On top of the lectern was a bible. Captain Mong had been walking behind him. Now he came and took the bible in his hands and held it out.

'Put your right hand on the bible,' he said. 'Raise your left hand in the air.'

The man put his right hand on the bible. It was a book and meant nothing to him. The leather was cool under his fingers. He raised his left hand in the air.

'Are you Frans Niemand,' said Captain Mong, 'minister of the mission church of – '

'No,' he said.

Silence in the church.

'Are you the Reverend Frans Niemand –'

'No,' he said. 'I'm not.'

Now into the silence a buzzing. In the choir-stall Valentine stood up and held the railing and sat down again. The judge rapped smartly with his gavel.

'Order,' he said. 'Order.'

Captain Mong turned to the judge. 'The minister has been sick,' he said.

'I'm not a minister,' he said.

Now the murmuring was words and somewhere somebody laughed. The man turned his head and for the first time looked at that audience which gave off sound without seeming to produce it just as bees do or water.

31

Then the back door of the church was kicked open and a man came running in. He was bawling out words that few people could make out except for the name of Captain Mong. There was consternation. The policeman and the newcomer held a whispered conversation and the policeman whispered to the judge and then the policeman ran out of the church. The judge struck again with the gavel. He said that the court was adjourned. Then a voice said All Rise and the judge went out and the people were left sitting in a stupor of amazement before they all began talking to each other. Someone had heard animal and someone had heard cage and someone else had heard the word escape.

32

'What kind?'
  'A lion.'
  'I heard a bear.'
  'There weren't any bears.'
  'It was a goat.'
  'He killed a goat?'
  'In the middle of the street.'
  'No, it was in the quarry. That's what I heard.'
  'It wasn't in the quarry.'
  'A goat? Why would he –'
  'It wasn't a goat.'
  'What was it?'
  'Whatever it was.'
  '*Ja*, whatever.'

33

Everybody in the court stood up and was moving around and everybody was speaking at once. Out of the bedlam a policeman emerged and went up to the prisoners. He was a policeman that none of them had seen before, a nameless person, arbitrary. He gestured to them to follow. Then he turned his back.

As Small walked out of the box Valentine bent and took from the inside of his sock the sharpened sliver of metal that had once been a spoon. It had been filed against the wall until its point was fine. Since the time that he had left the cell that morning it had rested flatly against the surface of his skin until it was as warm as his body and now he pushed it with surprising ease into the blue back of the policeman and the blue changed colour in an instant.

The policeman fell. Or he didn't fall but went down on his knees. He was trying to reach round behind him. To pull it out. Valentine went past him quickly and past his brother Small too. Through the opened door of the vestry. There were shirts and jackets hanging on a rack and a basket of little oddments and a safe set into the wall. A large single window looking out on a garden and he ran very hard at the glass. It gave way like water and he fell through its surface and was lying on leaves, amongst rock. All this seemed to happen without sound.

Valentine got up. There was soil and blood on his hands and glass lying everywhere like frost. He was dimly aware of a periphery of faces turned heavily towards him like sunflowers. He ran at the faces. They parted in front of him and drew back and he was at the head of a street that stretched away in diminishing perspective towards an invisible point. He ran towards the point. Houses went past on either side and gardens and kerbstones like loaves of white bread. Then there were no more houses but grass and stones on each side and he continued to run at the point that receded and the township rose in silence in front of him. He ran at the point and the point was the plaza and then the point was the church. The doors were open under the lopsided cross and there was no sound except the sound that he made and the point was inside the church. And he ran towards the vanishing point.

34

The church emptied quickly. Only he was left. He sat for a long time in the witness box. Then he got up and walked down through the nave of the church to the doors. Nobody arrested him, he was detained by nobody.

He walked down the street. In the houses with their naked brick faces the lights were going on like stars and from the gardens that he passed small plaster gnomes watched him, their colours pale from the sun and time, and he knew he was not part of any of this, it not part of him either.

He came to the edge of town. The last house, the last fence, and what unrolled away beyond that was what had always been here. The earth was hard and brown. Across it the road ran level as a plank. He took off the burned black robe and shed it there on the verge like a skin which no longer fit him. He walked.

He spent the night at the quarry. There was a rock over-hanging the edge and he curled up and slept on this like an innocent, a figure in a story not his. In the morning when he woke it was already full light. A procession was passing in the road. He walked a little way and watched. The wagons rode in file, tardy and tremendous, their wheels cutting tracks in the dirt. There were caravans and horses and midgets and girls and the cavalcade passed with tumultuous slowness. Some of them called to him but he didn't call back. He stood and watched them come over the ridge.

Then from the wagons he saw the rider appear on the machine, moving very fast. He was going back and forth between the vehicles. The man watched him with curiosity at first. The sound of the engine was tiny and metallic, the noise of a bee in a room. It was hard to see clearly in the glare and dust and only when he came closer could the man see what he was wearing.

Then he headed out along the edge of the quarry, leaving the road behind. He was running. The rider was perhaps five hundred metres distant and this was all that was between them as he resumed his journey on a morning still cold, still pale with a pure early light.

35

It ran as far as the wharf and when it came to the edge with the sea heaving darkly below it turned and tried to get past him but he was close behind it with his gun already drawn and he dropped to one knee and fired and missed and fired again and this time hit it in the side or the neck and it fell backwards kicking and into the sea and he ran to the edge and stood braced on the planks wet with weed and spray and it was rolling in the water below and he fired twice more for the crazed joy of it, the water upleaping to the kiss of the bullets and the sad carcass sinking from sight. He watched till it had vanished. He pushed the revolver back into its holster. It was hot like a hand on his hip. He walked slowly back down the wharf between the bollards and coils of rope to where a crowd had gathered near the road.

'Did you get it?'

'*Ja*. It's gone.'

'Captain Mong?'

'*Ja?*'

'One of the prisoners escaped. The other one tried too but he –'

He ran all the way back to the white church. Empty and desolate, its doors thrown open on darkness. He went in. The pews stood skewly and bibles and hymnbooks were scattered on the ground as if the place had been sacked. He came back out again running and only when he was halfway between the town and the township did he slow again to a walk. He was limping slightly and gasping. He sounded like an angry child crying. By this time it was night.

Before he reached the plaza he could see it. The glow was still soft and secretive but the smell was unmistakable. He knew. He swore in a quiet voice and started running again. He ran into the plaza. All around like dumbfounded junkies stood watchers with mouths hanging open.

He told them to form lines. They obeyed him. Buckets were passed hand to hand and when they reached the end of the line were emptied and sent back again. Then the fire-engine came. It was the only one in the town and it had last been used three years before. It drove into the plaza, bell dinning, one front tyre flat and all its hubcaps missing and a bird's nest built on its bumper. The driver was the only fireman. He jumped down, muttering and wall-eyed, frenetic. There was a ragged hose on the back. There was nothing to fix the hose to. The fireman stood cursing with the useless black hose and the lines of people who were passing the buckets stopped what they were doing and the buckets were put down on the concrete. Someone climbed up on the engine, the better to watch the conflagration. Others followed. In the end even the fireman sat up in his cab, eating a sandwich and watching.

How the little church burned. The bricks built up to astonishing heat and shattered in sudden explosions and the rafters groaned and shifted like bones and tiles slid and broke on the ground. The fire was like an envelope with a picture sealed inside it. Pigeons flew blinded by smoke and night and their shadows were punched out on the clouds overhead like ancient more terrible birds and one of them caught alight and flew burning in a long trajectory and fell. The glare was like noon. The plaza reflected it and people congregated along the edges were talking and shouting but no human voice could be heard only the voice of the fire. Smoke rose in long supple lines.

There was one man apart from the rest and that was the Captain. His face had been blackened by ash and his uniform was rumpled and dirty. Even his buttons were dulled. He moved up and down along the edge of the fire and he picked things up sometimes and then put them down again. A bucket. A stone. A shoe that somebody had discarded. He was saying words to himself. He turned at one point and she was standing there, the woman. They looked at each other without speaking and he knew that he wouldn't ever touch her again though he didn't understand why. He turned away from her. The fire was twinned and reflected in his eyes like some other fire burning in his brain.

He walked across the plaza. On the wall of sandbags outside the police-station three policemen were sitting and watching. When they saw him coming they stopped talking and when they saw his face they got to their feet uneasily and looked around.

'I want you to find him,' he said.

'Captain?'

'Find him and bring him to me.'

They went away.

In an hour they came back again. The fire had passed its height and the flames were subsiding in the ruins. But the pop and hiss of wood were audible behind him. He sat crouched down on his heels. He didn't stand up.

'He's not in town, Captain.'

'Someone saw him going south.'

'North.'

'South.'

'We can get dogs in the morning.'

'Dogs?' He blinked up at them, weary, confused. He looked old.

'To follow him, Captain. If we can give them a scent, from the blanket in the cell, maybe –'

Now he did stand. His face had cleared again. 'Who?' he said. His voice sounding quiet and thin.

They looked at him. 'The prisoner, Captain.'

'No,' he said. 'Not the prisoner.'

'Not the prisoner?'

He gestured behind him.

'Did the prisoner do this?'

They looked at the fire. They looked back at him. One of them looked down at the ground.

'I don't know, Captain.'

'Bring me the minister,' he said. 'It's the minister I want.'

When they came back again it was past midnight and the fire had burned down low. The watchers had mostly dispersed except for two or three at the far end of the plaza. Captain Mong was sitting on the wall of sandbags, staring in front of him.

'We can't find him, Captain. He's nowhere.'

'Look again,' he said. 'He's somewhere.'

'Captain, we've been all over the –'

'Look again,' he said.

This time they were gone for three or four hours. He didn't move from where he sat. It was dawn when they came back for the last time, their faces pinched and drawn with fatigue. They were carrying the cassock. He took it and held it up and shook it and asked them where they had found it. They told him and he nodded and thanked them and then he drew it over his head. They looked at him, astonished. He walked past them without looking at them.

In the fire-engine parked at the edge of the square the fireman was uncomfortably sleeping. He woke to an unfamiliar guttural sound and sat up in the cab. He saw the dark foundations of what had been a church with part of one wall somehow standing and through the fibrillations of heat still arising from it he saw a motorbike moving away.

'Now it's morning again,' he said.

As he went down the road out of the township the Captain

saw that the circus had gone. There was a bald place on the ground where the tent had been standing but no other remnant or sign. He rode slowly at first. Only when he had passed through the town and was on the road going out did he open up the throttle. The day was still and clear with a thin fur of dew on the grass. There were birds flying in cryptic formations overhead and once he saw a creature at the side of the road sitting vertically upright in surprise and then bolting away but he was otherwise the only living thing abroad. An emissary bearing bad tidings.

The road travelled straight into the sun and then swung and went up a ridge. The circus was here. The trucks and wagons were strung out in a line on the road. He didn't slow down as he got to them though he was going fast by now. The cage at the very back of the line was empty. He swung wide of it and around the front and wove his way between the vehicles like this all the way up the ridge. He came to the top. The road dropped away below with the line of wagons and cars continuing on it and the quarry was on the left. The bike lifted from the ground and hung and came down and he was moving between the radiators and the astonished faces and animals shying away behind bars. When the slope evened out he had almost drawn level with the quarry. He knew already what it was that he would see: the man the hole the man running

He went past the quarry and turned. The man was heading east, already some distance away. The policeman drove across the gravel with stones spraying out behind him and when he came to where the grass started he went on. He didn't know what he expected. That he would continue to ride where no road was. That nothing material could stop him. The bike went a short way and then it hit something and stopped. It bucked and keeled over and he went over the handlebars, performing an elaborate gymnastic in the air before he also hit the ground. He landed on his side with one arm extended and a large pain passed brightly across him.

When he sat up the world was moving like water and he could hear laughter from a distance. His bike lay nearby with oil dribbling out of it and its front wheel spinning around. He turned and looked back and along the road all the wagons had stopped and the people were laughing at him. Parked in a long line in the sun, gesticulating and jeering. He turned and looked the other way for the man but he wasn't where he had been. He was remote and diminished by distance. A tiny figure, going from him.

He stood up. His thigh felt stiff when it moved. There was a deep graze on his hand. He took the gun out of its holster. The laughter got louder and more raucous and someone shouted something at him. He turned and fired at them. Now there was one bullet left. The laughter stopped immediately and all along the wagons the watching figures dropped out of sight.

He yelled wordlessly back at them as he pushed the revolver back into its holster. He picked up a stone and threw it and it fell in an arc into the quarry. He heard it strike. He turned again and went after the man. He was hobbling and lurching. When he had gone a little way the people emerged from their wagons again to watch him. Somebody made a joke and a few of them laughed loudly and then the circus went on travelling down the road.

36

The man heard the shot behind him. It was distant and tiny, a door slamming far away somewhere. He was running already but he ran faster now though he didn't have the strength to sustain it. When he had gone a little way he stopped and looked back behind him. There was a commotion of some sort at the quarry. He could see the wagons strung out along the road, though they seemed to be stationary now, and a little centre of movement out in the veld from which a fine haze of dust was arising. He turned and ran on.

The distance between him and the quarry became quickly greater and greater. He ran out through the wasteland of grass as if he was being pursued. The sun was climbing now and the dew had dried from the grass and the air was stiffening with heat. He ran. He tripped in a hole once and fell but he got up without pausing and ran on. When he couldn't run any further he stopped and looked behind him again but he couldn't see anything except grass.

He went on, walking now. His body felt lessened, as if something had ebbed out of it. He had pains in his side and head. He breathed shallowly and fast and he found it hard to keep upright. The sun was hot. There were no clouds. At noon there was no shade anywhere. He stopped and stared around him and the landscape continued in a dry yellow sameness of grass. He walked towards what he thought was east but there was nothing to mark out any direction. Heat shimmered around him and the grass hissed softly. He imagined water and he thought about its clearness and he thought about the sounds water made.

He came to a large rock bulging out of the ground. He climbed up on to it to see. The rock was very hot and he couldn't touch it with his hands. He walked on it. He clambered up to the highest point and stood there, looking around. The earth seemed uniform and flat. He looked for the road but he didn't know in what direction it was. He turned a full circle, looking every way, before he stopped rigid and stared.

It was a long time before he was sure. In the desolation it might have been a termite hill, a branch. But it was a human figure moving slowly. He stood quite still, looking back, and then he sat down on the rock.

He breathed out. He stood up on the rock again and brought his hands up to his face. A big man, very tall. He went down the side of the rock that was farthest away from the policeman and started to run on through the grass. In a short time he slowed to a walk. He gasped for breath and kept looking behind him and his shoulders were trembling again. When he looked behind him now he saw the other man clearly, both of them bisected by the line of the grass, their halved bodies floating and bobbing.

The sun went down in a sewage of colour and the landscape looked violent and strange. At first the darkness was complete. The only light came from the stars. He thought he could change course in the night but the sky to his left grew paler and he could see the horizon and then the moon came up. It was full and round with a blue barren face and it cast its radiance down. The grass was like metal in the thin blue light and everything could be seen.

The heat of the day disappeared quickly. He could feel dew prickling on him. Then the moon set and then it was dark. He was very tired by now and his mind had no edges and twice he fell asleep on his feet. He staggered and caught himself and the third time he did fall, sprawling on his face on the ground. He fell asleep immediately and he didn't care what might happen to him.

He woke abruptly and tried to get up. He couldn't. He fell and clambered and fell over again. A baby. A drunk. He lay there and suddenly he laughed. The sound was harsh and not quite human to his ear, as if it came from somewhere outside him. He stopped laughing and looked around. The sun was up and there was a mist. The grass was weighted down with it and he bent his mouth to the drops and drank. He tried to stand again and this time he did.

He set off again, striking out randomly in the fog. After a short while the sun became hotter and the mist burned away and he could see the policeman behind him. He was further away than he had been yesterday but otherwise his pursuit was unchanged. A solitary figure plodding through the grass. Listing to one side like a sketch in a cartoon, a creature from which the stuffing was leaking. One man pursuing another man through the brown land. They were not people any more, they were a principle in operation: law and outlaw, hunter and quarry.

He came to a windmill which stood alone and skeletal in that ruined brown landscape like a monument to a deed done long ago and in the cracked concrete dam that stood at its base a thin gruel of slime had collected. He lay prostrate in it with his mouth pressed to the moisture. He drank. It tasted of sediments from deep in the ground but he drank it as if it were wine. He would have drunk bile, or blood. He felt the liquid move through him like a sort of emotion and his body took on a charge. He sat splay-legged in that primitive mud as if recently created from it and he gazed for a long time at his reflection in its surface with what was possibly amazement.

My face. My eyes. My mouth. When he got up again it was as if no time had passed but the sun was sinking in the west already and the earth was exhaling its heat. Far behind him he could see the policeman, advancing still, but slowly now, crippled, demented. His shape was elongated and wavering on the air like an abstract idea of a person.

The man climbed out of the dam and went on. When he had gone for a way he stopped and he saw the policeman come to the dam too and climb in. He experienced again the taste of the water because he knew that the other man was drinking. He sat down on the ground and waited. When the policeman climbed back out of the dam he got up again and went on. He was no longer sure that there was a difference between them or that they were separate from each other and they moved on together across the surface of the world and the sun went down and it got dark and still they continued in duet. They moved through the night in faintest silhouette like dreams that the soil was having.

He didn't sleep at all and when the sun came up again he was considerably weaker and the policeman had gained distance in the night. He was close enough now for his face to be visible and his buttons glinted like rivets.

He came to something that ran across his path and he stared in dull confusion at the parallel lines with their transverse slats of wood before his memory unpicked meaning in them. Train tracks. He looked at the line and then he followed it, one direction as good as another. The tracks ran on like sutures on the ground and he walked next to them. The earth was flat and barren still. But between the sleepers here and there he saw blades of grass growing. He passed a crushed beer-can and once there was a turd on the tracks. Towards noon of that day he heard a thin metallic humming. He thought it came out of his head. But the humming grew louder and it seemed to come from the ground and then it seemed to come from the tracks. He stopped and looked back. In the white heat and distance he saw the policeman, also stopped next to the tracks. Both of them standing there, waiting.

It came slowly, accreting rather than approaching, a speck becoming a shape and then a form growing quickly in speed. He stepped back and let it pass. It did pass. The engine was hissing and blotched with rust and he thought he saw two men moving in the cab but he wasn't sure and then the engine was gone and there was wind and the carriages were also going past. He stood stupefied and watched. Car after car after car with metal doors bolted and locked dragging past him in the dust and open platforms piled with pyramids of coal and wheat and one with a yellow car lashed down on it that was jouncing and sliding with the speed and then the carriages became more solid and discrete and their outlines more steady on the eye. There was a gushing sound and the friction of metal and the train was going much slower now. The wind eased and the groaning got softer and then the train stopped altogether. He looked to the left. Next to the track there was a tower of sorts and the engine was next to this tower. There was movement. He looked back in front of him. There was a box-car made of some brown rotting wood and the door in the side of it was open.

He climbed in. It was dark in the car. There were crates stacked up against the sides. In the gloom at the far end there was another human figure crouching. A ragged man in overalls, face hunted and haunted, eyes dark. Much like he was himself. They looked at each other and then the man leaned forward and looked along the line of carriages at the policeman. He watched him come closer and he continued to watch him even when the train jolted underneath him again and again started to move. The policeman made a clutching motion at the nearest car but there was no purchase and he stopped dead and stood with the dust swirling thickly around him. He receded quickly in the haze and the train was moving on, moving on.

Then the man sat back in the gloom. He looked at his companion. Now they recognized each other and after all that had taken place it didn't seem surprising that they should be reunited here. They still didn't speak but as the train went into a curve light fanned through the inside of the car and the two of them nodded to each other. Gravely, as passengers do. Then the train gathered speed and Valentine's head dropped in sleep and the man sat in the open rectangle of the door and he watched how the molten earth poured.

37

There was a box of matches left there for the candles with only one match in it. The flame was a tiny centre of light. He cupped a hand to keep it from dying. There is something in fire no matter how small that is the same as something in us and he looked for an instant into the flame as at some truth from his own life that he had suddenly understood and then he bent with it to the altar that was covered with a worn brocade. He broke a chair and fed it to the flames. In minutes the front of the church from where the minister had delivered his sermons was writhing with light and heat and thickening tendrils of smoke. He turned and ran to the door and out. He stopped only for a moment outside but the plaza was deserted and he ran across it to the northern end and stopped. He looked back and then he ran on.

He went through the streets of the township. Only when the houses ended and the veld began did he lift up his head. The ground was riven and dry. He came to a ditch with brown reeds growing in it and a worn plank laid across and he stopped again and looked behind him. The sky was clear but smoke zigged across it like a thin fatal flaw in something otherwise perfect and he ran over the plank across the ditch and on.

He went a long way that night without sleeping. He had burned one hand in the fire and when he woke at dawn he was in pain. There was a large blister in his palm like a weird white stigma and he tore a piece from his shirt to bind it. With his bandaged hand and his broken gait he limped on over the land.

By mid-morning he saw a line of blue mountains off to his right, very small, very distant, a stain seeping up from the horizon. They were geometric and featureless, a graph of some kind. He altered course and went towards them. They drew him.

By nightfall they were closer. The sun went down but the tiny peaks ahead glowed red and faint like a filament cooling long after the sky had gone dark. Then they also went out.

He came to a farmhouse and orbited warily around it. Then he went closer. There was a washline strung between two poles with a pair of overalls hanging on it. He took the overalls for himself and left his own clothes in their place, flapping ragged and hollow from the wire. There was a well nearby and he winched the metal bucket to the surface and drank the dark water in it. Cool water, earthsmelling. He looked around till he found an old bottle and filled it with the water and went on. Later he found an anthill that was partly hollowed out and he crawled into the chamber and lay down. He slept encased in mud that was crenellated with tunnels like a brain.

At dawn he woke and stretched and set off at a slow run. The mountains rose out of the level plain ahead as sudden as an accident and by noon he was in their foothills. He was diminished and pared by the high peaks, the gorges. He came to a stream. He drank and took off his clothes and washed in it. The water was cold and brilliant on his skin and it continued to ache in him long after he had left it behind. He went on up the steepening ground while the shadow over him became deeper and at dusk he came to a copse of trees and crawled among their dark boles and slept. He woke at first light among a matrix of roots and it was a full minute before he knew where he was.

He wandered on among the outcrops, going higher and higher. He came to a footpath. He followed the path. He passed a scarlet lizard with a ruff of skin around its neck. He saw a snake sliding through a crevice. He passed a white bone lying next to the path that might have come from any creature's body, his body. In the afternoon he came to the ridge. The path went over it and down and he saw a valley opening out with a cluster of houses in it. A train track running down from the houses. He crouched behind the rocks to wait.

At twilight he descended, skulking from shadow to shadow like a villain. It was full dark when he came to the houses. In an iron bin overflowing with refuse he found the remains of a meal and he ate ravenously, like a dog, crusts bones skin potatoes beans.

Afterwards he passed along the outskirts of the little settlement till he came to the railway track glimmering faintly. Standing on it in a prolonged procession of inert formations was an engine and a line of carriages. He walked along them and back again. There was nobody else nearby. On the door of one of the cars the padlock was rusted and he used a branch and the remains of his strength to force it to open for him. Crawled in. He lay in the dark and comfort of odours and he thought that he would leave before daylight.

But the sun had cleared the rim of the mountains already when he woke and the train was rocking like a boat. He stood in the doorway and saw the village, the drab houses, backsliding. Then the train gathered speed and he heard it under him and he heard the echo returning. He sat against the wall of the carriage and slept again and woke, slept and woke. He saw the mountains recede like a bite-mark on the sky and then a charred plain replaced them. Outside the train there was nothing. He slept more and when he woke the train was stopping and then a man climbed up into the car.

38

He said a word to his companion.

Valentine looked strangely at him. He mimed the action of drinking. Valentine gestured to a crate. He saw that the crate had been opened. He crawled to it and inside it and maybe inside all of them were bottles filled with bright yellow cooldrink and he took one and opened it and drank.

He drank another and another and another. He and his ragged companion sat hunkered in the open door together, drinking bottles dry and discarding them. They threw them out of the door and they burst on the ground in tiny and beautiful explosions. There was nothing to eat in the car. He had an urge to take the other man's hand and because he wanted to he did so. Then they crouched there together like lovers, not looking at each other, not speaking.

The sun went down. The train moved through the dark and he saw flames spurting up from the wheels. He saw the burned-out carapace of a car standing in the wilderness where no road was. He fell asleep as if a switch had been thrown in his head and when he opened his eyes again he was lying on his back and Valentine had retreated to his corner and was crying out in his dreams. *Nee broeder*, he called, *moenie moenie*. He sat up and looked out through the doorway and they were passing through a bare stony country with low hills, thin scrubby bushes. He saw a fence made of barbed wire and sheep following each other like people and the train passed howling through a settlement of tin shacks between which were men women children standing staring or running after the train and the wind of its passage made their fire lean backward and sparks flew up on the air. Then the dark clapped down like a hand as if they had never been. He staggered to his feet and pissed out the door into the world. The first time in three days. He lay again and was again instantly asleep as if a blind had dropped in his brain and he dreamed about a woman that might have been his mother or perhaps she was some other woman.

When he woke again the train was juddering to a stop. The sky through the door was light. He crawled to the crate and took two more bottles out. The other man was sleeping in the corner with his face pressed against the wood. He nodded to his back and when the train had stopped completely he climbed out of the car. The train was standing at a siding and there were other carriages and other tracks nearby and a line of low buildings in the distance and the smell of the sea on the air.

He went towards the buildings. They looked shuttered and barred but there were people moving around between them who didn't pay him any mind and he went around them to the back. There was a marsh here with beyond it a town of some kind. He saw streets and windows and cars moving and he set out across the marsh. Mud sucked at his feet, reeds were sibilant around him. When he came to the other side he was smeared in the primeval murk and encased in it up to the knees.

He thought at first he was in a city. There were so many people in the streets and cars parked everywhere at angles. Then he saw that the people were here for some reason. They stood around in groups and some of them had cameras in their hands or mounted on tripods and some of them were holding pieces of blackened glass that looked insanely beautiful to him. They were looking up into the sky and he also looked up but he could see nothing in it.

He was very hungry now and he wandered through the

dusty streets looking for food. He didn't know where he was but he supposed that all towns were alike. Only after he had stumbled its length for an hour did he look up and see the spire of a church and something in it, the angle or shape, arrested him. He went closer. He stood astounded, looking up. He went closer again and when he stood on the blue slate outside he cast around him wildly as if something had been lost. He seemed about to cry. But he didn't cry. He stood still and looked around at the town and then he dropped to one knee for a moment and got up.

39

In the wilderness in the night the policeman came to the top of a rise and saw a farmhouse below him, tiny and square with lighted windows and smoke rising from a chimney like a small child's dream of a house, and he hesitated only a moment before he came staggering down the slope towards it. As he came closer he saw an old black man in old clothes chopping wood at the back and the old man stopped chopping and stood with his axe in his hands and stared. A huge inbred dog got up from the shadow at the side of the house and ran at him, barking. A chain pulled it back as it lunged and he passed while it yearned with its mouth. He went in through the back door. A kitchen with a wooden table with a family sitting around it. A man, a woman, two daughters. They sat with knives and forks in their hands and stared slack-jawed and stricken at this apparition that had entered their lives. Ragged and reeking like the survivor of some ultimate catastrophe.

He pulled up a chair at the table and sat down. There was a meal piled up on plates waiting to be served, food wrested from branches, from under the ground, from inside the bodies of animals. He reached out with his filthy, his bloody hands and began to eat without looking at them. Such was his hunger, such was his need.

He didn't notice the commotion and the fleeing around him but at some point he looked up and saw overturned chairs and the room empty except for the glowering face of the farmer. Two barrels pointed at him.

'No,' he said, still chewing.

'What no?' said the farmer. 'What no?'

'I'm with you,' Captain Mong said. He was gnawing a piece of chicken and he laid a fine bone down on the edge of his plate. 'I'm the law,' he said, wiping his mouth. 'I'm with you.'

In the morning the farmer took him home. The two daughters stood hand in hand outside to wave him goodbye. The farmer drove down rutted tracks scarcely discernible to the eye and through gates that stood in the desolation to mark the entrance to nothing and in time they came to a road and that road led to another. Hours had gone past by now. Then he saw where he was. The road came to the quarry and went past it and over a ridge and on and there were other cars on the road, all of them going towards the town.

He said, 'What is it? What's going on?'

The farmer looked at him and shrugged.

'The cars. Where is everybody going to?'

'I don't know,' said the farmer.

All along the streets of the town there were cars parked and people walking and the commotion was charged as if an event was imminent. The farmer dropped him in the main street. They said goodbye and shook hands and said they hoped to see each other again but they didn't and then the farmer was gone.

The policeman went in search of the doctor. He found him in his office near the wharf. The doctor made him take off his clothes. He lay naked on the cool table while the doctor peered and prodded at his body with his fingers and the tips of his tools. Lift your arm, he said, lift up your leg. Turn over.

'What's happening outside?' he said. 'Why are all the people here?'

The doctor straightened up. 'It's the eclipse today,' he said.

'The eclipse.'

'This is the centre of it.'

'Oh,' said the policeman.

'Does it hurt when I push here?'

He came out of the doctor's office trussed-up and bandaged like a birthday present. He had a cracked rib and a torn ligament and a variety of bruises on his body. The little finger on his left hand was broken. He smelled bad even to himself. He limped all the way to the white church and past it along the road to the township. Everything looked different to his eyes but it may have been the quality of the light.

He came to the plaza. The blackened shell of the church stood at one end but he averted his eyes from it. His motorbike was standing outside the wall of sandbags in the place where it always stood. But it didn't look the way that it had. The paint was scarred and scuffed and the front tyre was shredded and spokes stood out as if in shock. He went past it and the sandbags into the charge office at the front with its counter and the pimply boy sitting behind it.

The boy looked at Captain Mong as if he were famous or dead.

The Captain went past him too and into his own office and looked around at the desk and the noticeboard and the cabinet and the picture of Jesus on the wall. He went around behind his desk and sat. The glass bowl was there like a gypsy's crystal ball but the goldfish was floating on its back. The Captain stared into the transparent globe as if his fortune were indeed revealed there and then he dipped his fingers into it and retrieved the fish with distaste. He held it by the edge of its tail. He looked at it and then he flung it up and it hit the roof and stuck there. In time it hardened like a fossil.

A few minutes later a policeman came into the office. There was a threadbare place in the carpet which other feet had worn down and the policeman stood here too. 'Captain – ' he said.

Captain Mong didn't look up. 'Can nobody feed the fucking fish,' he said. 'It's only been three days.'

'Captain, they've got him. We've just heard. In the town.'

Now he did look up, eyes brilliant and steady. 'Got who?'

'The prisoner, Captain.'

He dropped his eyes again. 'The prisoner,' he said. He looked tired.

'They've got him down at the café in the main road.'

'*Ja*,' he said. '*Ja*.'

'Are we going to get him, Captain? Or must we –'

'*Ja*,' he said again. '*Ja*.'

The strips of light coming in through the blinds were diminishing steadily in power.

40

'The darkest place in the world.'
    'Here?'
    'On this side. On the other side it's night.'
    'Here?'
    'When?'
    'Now. The light's going already, you can see.'
    'I can't see.'
    'Look.'
    'I can see.'
    'Look!'
    'Is it him?'
    'What?'
    'It is. Look at him. It is.'
    'Where?'
    'There. What's the matter with him?'
    'Who? Who? Who?'
    'It's him.'
    'What's the matter with him?'
    'Let's get him.'
    'With what? What with?'
    'With this.'
    'And this.'
    'Let's get him.'
    'Yes.'
    'Come.'
    'Yes.'

41

Valentine woke alone in the box-car with a regular metallic gonging sounding in his ears from somewhere. He drank down a bottle of the bright yellow cooldrink and pocketed another for later. He climbed down out of the car. There was a man a little distance away who was bent down at the wheels of the engine and striking at them with a hammer. Valentine went past the mad musician and on. The siding was in an empty lot that was rank and thick with weeds and he walked across several rows of tracks that crossed each other crazily like ladders piled up and went through a hole in the fence. There was a flat marsh in front of him and beyond it a town sketched thinly on the sky. He went towards the town.

There were weeds with plumed tips like brushes but the sky had no colour in it. He came out of the marsh into the street. It was a town like the town he had lived in but also like no town he'd seen. The light that came down was diffused and spectral and the outlines of buildings unclear. The air was still and dead and hot as if in the aftermath of lightning.

There was something in Valentine that was altered. He carried his head like a beaker filled with water and indeed his eyes were liquid and centreless. He came slowly down the pavement with his exaggerated gait and when he came to the corner opposite the café he stopped. He stood there on the corner, shaking his head and looking around.

He had been there for three or four minutes when the people came out of the café. There were four men and two women and they advanced on him in a phalanx. One of them was carrying a crowbar and one of them had a stick. He thought that one other had a gun. He watched their progress with interest. They came over the street and up on to the pavement towards him. They moved with purpose and they encircled him and took hold of him with their hands. They were speaking harshly to him though their voices seemed wordless and their faces were hard with their thoughts. He went with them across the street to the café and the light was greatly lessened by now.

42

He walked away from the white church down a side-street but there were people a little way ahead on the pavement and he turned again and went back. He went down another street. He went only a little way before he sat down abruptly on the kerb and bowed his head suddenly into his hands.

He sat there quite still for a minute and then he stood up again and walked with intent. He went round the side of the white church. The road to the township ran on level and straight with grass on either side.

He walked to the west of the road to avoid people travelling on it. He went north towards the township. In the dead place where the circus tent had been there was a family sitting in deck-chairs around a blanket. The mother looked curiously at him with a black ring around her eye from the burnt glass she was holding. He went past. As he came closer to the township he walked more warily till on the outskirts he paused. There was a boy in the road throwing a tennis ball up and catching it. He called the boy over to him. They spoke briefly. He asked the boy if he knew the woman and the boy said that he did. He asked him to call her. The boy said that he would and he fumbled through his pockets for payment but he didn't own anything to give. In the end he held out one of the bottles of cooldrink and the boy took it and walked away between the houses.

He waited for fifteen minutes before he knew the boy wasn't returning. He sat down again where he was to consider. He spoke a few words softly to himself. Then he got up again and walked in the direction that the boy had gone in, walking between the houses, going slowly. The light had thickened greatly by now.

He came to the edge of the plaza midway between the police-station and the house. He looked at the police-station but the sandbags and the hanging flag were static and he could see nobody outside. He looked the other way to the church. The church was gone. He looked at the rubble strewn and blackened and the single charred wall with its irregular edge and the footprints crossing hither and thither. He looked for a long time and then he raised one hand to the side of his head and dropped it.

He looked at the house. It was closed. The door and the window were closed and in the room that he'd slept in the curtains were drawn. There was an acre of concrete between him and the house and he looked at the police-station and at the house again but there was nobody outside either.

Then a hand pulled at his shirt. He turned. It was a woman. There was another woman with her. They began to remonstrate with him in a language different to his and the first woman kept pulling at his shirt. He stared at them without comprehending. Then one of them gestured to the church and he understood that they were two of the faithful.

He took a step back. 'No,' he said. 'No.'

They continued to talk. He sensed a hunger in them but he didn't know what it was. He moved away from them. He went back down between the houses to the grass and walked across the grass to the road. There was another figure coming down the road from the township and when they saw one another both stopped. They stood very still in the unnatural dusk and looked at each other in the road.

43

they herded him into a corner of the shop between shelves of tins and magazines piled up and fridges humming, they leered at him, they shouted, one of them prodded him with a stick. a crowbar. one of the others was using a telephone. their voices chafed around him. he found a clear place on the floor and sat down. on the shelf that was level with his head there was a box of biscuits and he opened it, hands shaking. inside were lurid rectangles of pink blue white with animal shapes stamped out in icing on them and he ate three before he was seen.

then he was beaten. by a woman. her face was transfigured with a fury of which he was not the real object and she lashed at him with the stick while screaming out vile imprecations as if the biscuits were unspeakably priceless. every blow that landed made dust squirt out of him in jets. he tried to shield himself at first but the blows were distant and unreal. the stick broke. the top of it spun away into a corner and the woman bounded fiendishly behind it.

he leaned on one of the shelves to get up and it broke. tins and newspapers slid and splashed to the floor and he walked backwards from the gathering chaos. horrified. he went to the door. when he got there he started to vomit. pinkwhiteblue coming out of him in spurts like the ghastly essence of himself. he staggered out in the crimson twilight and started to go down the road.

then the voices rose baying like a mad chorus and they were running behind him in a thicket of flesh, many-armed multi-eyed ravenous

44

He turned away from the policeman and started to run down the road towards the town. The policeman started running behind him. They went very quickly down the level straight road with the light ebbing steadily around them. Even the birds had gone silent

45

and clutching and dragging and pulling at him he broke free
of them and ran up the main street between the solemn assem-
bly of watchers sitting in their chairs lying on their backs
standing their telescopes and cameras and fragments of
coloured glass pressed to their eyes and the light was the light
of some other planet with a dwarf star for a sun cooling
slowly to an ember whole continents and seas below sealed up
in ice preserved in the layered gloom that might have
emanated from him he ran in all the thick hot stillness he was
the only point of motion of frenzy

46

He ran past the white church and on. He ran down a road that joined another road that went into the main street. He ran down the middle of the street. It was almost full dark by now but the windows at the edge of the street were lit and silhouetted against them were the outlines of people squatting or lying or crouching in postures that seemed to betoken something but what. It felt that his whole life had been expended in motion, had consisted of no substance but flight

47

The policeman ran behind in his befouled and bespattered uniform and his pristine white bandages and the ruined cassock overall and while he ran he tried to pull his gun from the holster with one bullet left in it to fire

48

And ahead of him in the street he saw somebody running towards him. He couldn't slow down or change direction so he continued to run as he was. Very straight, very fast. The other man was to one side of him, to the right, and they passed each other in the weird red dusk, both of them running at speed. If they knew each other it wasn't spoken. He ran on and to his right there passed a collection of people in pursuit of the other man running. He saw their faces demented and yearning for blood and one of them clutched at him and then he was past. He ran on down the road. He passed the lighted window of the café on one side with shelves of goods visible behind it and then a butchery and a hair salon and then there was a darkness ahead from which came the susurration of the sea. There was a metal boom across the road. He started veering to go around the boom. When the shot came he didn't hear it entirely, just the first edge of the report that seemed to slice off suddenly in the air and in the silence on the far side of it he was falling as if through measureless space.

The metal boom hit his cheek. Then the ground. He lay there in the road with his face pressed down to the tar and with his last strength remaining pushed down with his hands. Rolled over. He saw the sky with stars burning in it and the policeman's head outlined against them. The sun was a dark disc punched out on the sky with one fiery rim still protruding and then it went out

49

the darkness was sudden and complete and it came as he drew
opposite a house there was a low fence a gate he went in
through the gate there was a dustbin and he crouched down
beside it on the far side of the fence in some other world altogether he heard the cries and footfalls of pursuit grow louder
and then diminish and taper he moved still at a low crouch
from the dustbin down the length of the wall he went down
the side of the house like a blind man reading braille with his
fingers there was a wall here another gate he went through
and on through another garden another street and on

50

'He's gone.'
  'I thought I saw –'
  'No, he's gone.'
  'Somebody ran the other way.'
  'Was it him?'
  'Look everywhere. Look more. Look, look.'
  'He's gone.'
  'What about that other one running?'
  'That was somebody else.'
  'Are you sure?'
  'How do you know?'

51

The body lay in the road next to the metal boom for less than five minutes in all. Then somebody brought a stretcher. They loaded it on to the stretcher with its face looking up and hands hanging loose at its sides. There wasn't a lot of blood. Somebody else brought a blanket and they threw it over the body and two youths were conscripted to carry it. The little cortège went slowly down the street, Captain Mong limping ahead. Along the sides of the road the spectators gathered to watch and it was as if somebody important was gone and they had come to pay homage. The procession went all the way up the main street and through two side roads past the church. On along the road to the township. They moved very slowly and the sun came back quickly and by the time they reached the plaza it was light.

52

She came out of the house with her suitcase in her hand. She was wearing jeans and a shirt. She put the suitcase down for a moment. She closed the door behind her and stood with her hands on her hips, looking around. The plaza. The sandbags. The blackened foundations with the part of one wall left standing. There was a boy playing with a tennis ball in the rubble, throwing it up and catching it. When he saw her he stopped and watched her. After a moment he came over.

'There was another uncle,' he said. 'He was looking for you.'

'Oh,' she said. 'Today?'

'No,' the boy said. 'I think it was another day.'

She looked through her pockets for money and took out a coin. She gave it to him. He walked away holding it. She watched the tiny figure diminish till distance had consumed it entirely. There were other children playing and they stood up with ashened faces and looked at her. She picked up the suitcase and walked stiffly away over the plaza. The sound of her feet on the concrete became softer and softer and then she came to the edge of the plaza and her feet made no sound at all. She disappeared between buildings, walking fast.

53

In the cell at the edge of the plaza Small lay on the bed on his back. He had been lying in this position for some hours now, hands clasped on his stomach and the heels of his feet placed together. He was looking up at the ceiling.

In the ceiling he could see a face that had been made by water long ago. It was indistinct and distorted but he could see in it the places for eyes nose and mouth and he had projected a nature upon it. He stared intently at the face. He didn't move at all except to breathe. It was hot in the cell but as the afternoon went by it became gradually cooler and the sunlight that slanted in moved from the bed to the wall.

He had written his name on the wall.

Then the sun faded and it started to get dark and he couldn't see the face any more. Still he lay there on the bed, not moving. The electric light came on overhead and he shifted his position abruptly. He crossed one leg over the other leg and placed his hands at his sides. Valentine. Where are you Valentine.

54

He was walking at the edge of a tar road that ran like a stripe from horizon to horizon. The land was flat. The road went south across the flat land. He came along walking slowly, dragging his feet, and every now and then he would stop completely and stand there looking around. Then he started walking again.

Later when he heard a car behind him he moved off the road into the grass and crouched down till the car had gone past. When he stood up again he was holding a broken parasol that he'd found in the grass. He walked out into the road with it, turning it round in his hands, looking at it.

It was buckled and tattered but it opened and he held it over him and walked in its shadow. He held it in his left hand because the right still hurt from the fire. The cloth had come off and the blister was weeping in the centre of his palm like a religious marking of some kind. He himself looked crazed and messianic in his rags and his filth and his hair. He had only been on the road for three days but already he had taken into himself some of its logic, its lore. His sole destination was motion. He was thinner and stronger than he had used to be. There was a certain look in his eye.

55

He was buried in an unmarked grave in the corner of the graveyard next to the body of the minister. There was no service and nobody came to mourn. The coffin was a plain pine box and it was delivered to the cemetery in the morning by two policemen in a van. They carried it, cursing and slipping, to where the grave had been dug. They lowered the coffin on ropes and pulled the ropes out of the hole and went.

Then the gravedigger called Jonas got up from the flat rock where he'd been sitting and started to fill in the hole. He had been doing this job for thirty-seven years with unvarying punctiliousness and diligence. The graves were all the same depth and took the same time to dig and to fill. When he had finished he beat the earth flat with the back of the spade and propped up the spade against a tree. He went back to the flat rock and sat. He took tobacco out of his overall pocket and rolled a cigarette for himself. He was in the warm sunlight, smoking, looking out on the little crosses in the ground.

56

In the middle of the day everything in the quarry is lit from above by the sun. The boulders, the tiny trees, the vine growing up the cliff-face. All still and clear, static and visible. Nothing moves in the quarry.

Maybe a grasshopper flickers. Maybe a bird flies over, calling.

As the sun gets lower a shadow starts to go across it, beginning at one wall and spreading slowly across to the other. It climbs, filling up the quarry from below in much the way that water would. It is blue and cool, this shadow, and nothing is hidden by it yet. Only softened.

Then the sun goes down and the shadow in the quarry changes. It gets darker and objects are slowly lost in it, their outlines erased and consumed. The shadow thickens. Then it isn't shadow any more. It's darkness and the darkness in the hole is no different to the darkness above it but you can't see down into the quarry. It was dug a long time ago and it goes down deep into the ground. There might be water in the quarry, or movement, or nothing. There might be no bottom to it.